THE BONING KNIFE

THE BONING KNIFE

Hilda Stahl

Victory House, Inc.
Tulsa, OK

Published by
Victory House, Inc.
P.O. Box 700238
Tulsa, Oklahoma 74170
(918-747-5009)

Chapter 1

"You got to go, Beebe," she said, He laughed at the special nickname that she called him only when she wanted him to know how much she loved him. They sat at the kitchen table over cups of hot honey water. She wasn't supposed to drink coffee or tea.

Outside the wide window in back of the table, snowflakes danced in the air, but melted the minute they touched the ground. It was early April, a time when the weather couldn't decide on rain or snow.

"I got my walker and I got this thing." She patted the special necklace around her neck with the emergency button on it. She hadn't wanted to spend his hard-earned money on the Vital Call System, but he'd been so stubborn about it that she'd finally given in.

He saw the firm set of her jaw and the determination in her brown eyes behind her glasses. He didn't notice that her skin sagged or that she had deep wrinkles. He had loved her the last twenty years of their marriage. The first twenty-five he'd lived with her, had children with her, but had gone about his life pretty much the way he wanted to do.

Then one day he realized that she was important to him, and he suddenly wanted to make up for all the years when he'd stepped out on her or treated her badly. He sighed heavily. "All right, Cake." He'd nicknamed her Honey Cake, but long ago had dropped the Honey. "I'll get Aimee, but I hate to leave you alone."

"Aimee needs you."

He sighed. "I know." Last month Aimee had accidently learned that he was her natural father. She couldn't handle it and had driven away from town in anger. She'd thought her mother was a saint. Last night Aimee had called, broke and alone and in need of help. He'd said he'd find a way to get her and take her back to college so she could graduate in May the way she'd planned. She'd said she wanted him to come so they could talk out their relationship. Finally he'd agreed. "But I still wish I didn't have to leave you, Cake."

"I'll be all right." She touched the special necklace. "You drive careful. The roads could be slippery."

He kissed her soft lips, then kissed her again. "I love you."

"I love you, Beebe."

He lifted his hat and coat off the hook beside the back door, slipped his coat on over his carefully pressed blue shirt, then clamped his hat on his gray head. "I'll try to be back no later than noon tomorrow."

"I'll be fine."

"I wish there was somebody we could call to check up on you."

"I don't need to be checked up on. I got *this!* Now, get!"

He winked at her and walked out.

She sipped the last of her honey water and eased up out of her chair, careful to grip the walker firmly.

Several minutes later a pain shot up her arm, the same kind of pain she'd had when her heart had first started acting up. The strength left her arm and she staggered, flipped the walker and crumpled to the floor. Her head spun and blood pounded in her ears. Was this it?

Finally the pain eased and she pushed the special button to send the signal to the receiver beside the phone. Now, she'd have help. Soon she'd be just fine. They said it would only take a few minutes for help to arrive. She could hang on that long.

The clock ticked and the house creaked. Outside a car honked.

An hour later her back hurt from lying on the cold floor. She moved slowly, carefully, trying to ease herself up to crawl to the couch. Suddenly another pain ripped through her. She died with her finger on the special button.

Chapter 2

"Just look at that rain!" Carolynn Burgess said in a voice that she managed to keep light and bubbly. She'd wanted to say, "Don't be angry at me, Robert, but listen to me." She knew she'd have to lead up to it, not blurt it out over Thursday morning breakfast. "But that's what we can expect in April in Michigan, isn't it?"

She'd forced down her egg, toast and tea while Robert ate his usual bowl of corn flakes. "But it's supposed to quit before noon, then be partly sunny the rest of the day." She pulled her gaze from the kitchen window, looked across the breakfast table, and watched Robert fill his glass with Diet Pepsi. She didn't expect a response to her observation. He had always been a man of few words. Yet he had a quiet strength and had been a hard worker during his years of building houses. He'd provided a nice income for the family and had always been a good father to Eleena, Christa, Wesley and Stan.

Carolynn glanced around the comfortably large kitchen. Robert hadn't built the two-story, Cape Cod house, but his touches were in the new kitchen cupboards made of red oak, the hardwood floor, and he'd even put up the flowered wallpaper with some help from her. She'd chosen the color scheme — almond, medium-blue and dusty-rose.

She glanced across the round oak table at Robert. Just as soon as he drank his Pepsi she'd tell him the secret she'd kept from him throughout their marriage, that she'd done undercover work for Dumars Investigative Services even though Robert had thought she was working as Dud Dumar's part-time secretary, not full-time since Robert had insisted her place was at home with the children.

She had the credentials to become a licensed detective, but because of Robert and the children, she hadn't done so. Dud Dumars had said she had special skills that he could use from time to time, and she'd agreed to do undercover work for him. She'd made the decision to tell Robert the truth two weeks ago after she'd read a book on relationships and the importance of sharing yourself with your spouse, but she hadn't found the courage to do so until today.

She'd prayed for the right words and for the strength to share her secret with Robert. She looked at her faded jeans, the loose-fitting, red flannel shirt and white sneakers. Maybe she should've put on her new green blouse. With an unsteady hand she pushed back her dyed dark blonde hair, which had been medium brown before it had turned gray. Her eyes were blue and her face unlined and lightly tanned from spending time working in her flower garden and playing outdoors with their grandchildren.

Robert took a long drink of his Diet Pepsi. The past few years he'd taken to drinking soda for breakfast instead of coffee or juice as he had during the early years of their marriage. Carolynn had complained at first, then had given up because she knew once he'd made up his mind, nothing could sway him — not her anger or her pleading.

Robert sighed heavily, gulped down half a glass of soda, then leaned back in his chair. Deep lines fanned out from the corners of his dark eyes to his gray hair. He wore Levis, wide green suspenders and the green plaid shirt Carolynn had bought him last month. He didn't want to hear what she had to say, but he knew she had something on her chest and he knew he'd have to listen even if he didn't want to. She talked enough for the both of them. "I got three birdhouses to finish," he finally said with a scowl that made his dark brows almost meet over his large nose.

Carolynn's stomach knotted. Suddenly she lost the important words. He would be *so* angry! She locked her icy hands in her lap. "Robert, I want you to listen and not storm off to the basement."

His heart jerked. Was she going to tell him it was over? His friend Mack had been married almost fifty years when Lorna suddenly decided she couldn't stay with him any longer. They had divorced, breaking Mack's heart, but leaving Lorna free to pursue the life she wanted. Maybe Carolynn was tired of him, wanted out to lead a different life. Maybe she wanted to develop the singing career she'd always wanted. He'd known something was wrong between them for a long time, but he'd never found the courage to get to the bottom of it. He frowned at her. "You never did want me to take so much time with my birdhouses."

"I never said that!"

"You thought it!"

She shrugged. She had thought it. He buried himself away in the basement to build his birdhouses even when she wanted time with him. She'd looked forward to his retirement, hoping it would help them get back the passionate love they'd had the first few years of their marriage. "This is very hard, Robert. Please, don't blow up."

His jaw tightened. With God's help he'd learned to control his temper with his children, the people at work, but never with Carolynn. She always managed to rub him the wrong way at the wrong time.

"Robert, I've been...." Before she could tell him about her secret work with Dumars Investigative Services, someone knocked on the back door that was in the laundry room just off the kitchen. Relieved, she jumped up. "I'll get it."

Robert's hand trembled as he downed his Pepsi, then poured himself a little more. Maybe he wouldn't have to hear her news. He rubbed an unsteady hand over his sunken cheek. Did she want a divorce even though they were both Christians and didn't believe in divorce? He prided himself on understanding people, but he could never understand Carolynn. She always seemed just beyond his reach.

He had never understood why she'd married him. She was outgoing, talkative, and loved to be around people. He was content to come home from work and be with his family, or maybe get together with church friends from time to time. He closed his eyes and groaned.

Carolynn opened the door to find her daughter-in-law Kate standing there in the rain with four-year-old Heidi and two-year-old Carolynn, nicknamed Caro. Kate was short and slender with black hair and dark brown eyes. Before Carolynn could speak, Kate pushed inside, spraying out tiny drops of rain water. She pulled off Caro's pink spring jacket and dropped it over the clothes dryer.

"Mom, I know this is asking above and beyond, but I need to get some extra party balloon orders made up this afternoon and the kids are underfeet with this rain and all." Kate had started her own party balloon business a year ago in her home and was doing very well at it. She specialized in arranging gifts inside the large balloons. "Just until four this afternoon! Please!"

Carolynn sighed, then smiled down at Heidi and Caro, then at Kate. Now she had a reason not to tell Robert her secret until later. "I'll watch them, Kate."

"I figured you'd be glad for something to do on such a miserable day."

Carolynn knew her family thought she led a very boring life with no outside interests except her singing, her garden in the summer and her time with her grandchildren. None of them knew of the time she spent solving crimes, tracking down killers or finding missing persons. At times she almost burst with the desire to tell them about her other life, but she'd kept the carefully guarded secret.

"Grandma," said Heidi, clutching at Carolynn's shirttail as she looked up at her with wide, dark eyes. "Where's grandpa?"

"In the kitchen."

Without another word, Heidi, with her long brown hair flipping around her thin shoulders, ran to the kitchen to Robert.

Caro chattered her baby talk and lifted her arms to Carolynn to be held. Laughing, Carolynn picked her up and smelled the clean aroma of shampoo.

"You know their routines, mom," said Kate, kissing Caro, then squeezing Carolynn's arm. "See you at four."

Carolynn nodded as Kate rushed out into the April rain that had turned to drizzle. Her car was parked in the paved driveway beside the house.

"Cookie," Caro said with a smile that showed off the dimple in her right cheek.

"I'll give you a piece of toast," Carolynn said with a laugh. "No more of that 'cookie' business, little girl, and you know it. You can't wrap me around your little finger. I'm not your grandpa or your uncle Stan." Both men gave the grandchildren, especially the little girls, anything they wanted.

In the kitchen Carolynn set Caro in the high chair she'd brought from the attic for her grandchildren. Robert sat in his chair with Heidi on his knee. She was sipping his Diet Pepsi.

"So much for talking," Carolynn said lightly, carefully hiding her relief.

Robert shrugged, then set Heidi on his chair, walked out of the kitchen to the basement door in the hallway. He was glad Carolynn had been interrupted. Maybe now he'd have a chance to prepare himself for the worst. He frowned as he walked down the steps that he always kept tidily swept.

The basement was his to keep clean and he kept it in ship-shape form, free of cobwebs and dust. It might be better to know exactly what Carolynn had wanted to say. Maybe then he could decide on the action to take. He would not let her walk out on him! He groaned. "Please, Jesus, don't let her leave me."

Several minutes later Carolynn sat in her maple rocker and watched Heidi and Caro as they played on the den floor, toys scattered all around them. An ivy and a creeping Charlie hung from a plant tree at the side of the window. A Boston fern sat on a small round table beside the bookcase that Robert had built years ago. The floor was covered with a blue-gray, sculptured carpet and the walls were painted an off-white and were covered with framed family photographs.

Pursing her lips, Carolynn leaned back in her rocker. Maybe she wouldn't have to tell Robert about her work. After all, Dud hadn't called her on a case for about two months. Maybe he wouldn't call her. But what if he did? How could she get out of telling Robert the truth? Suddenly she knew. The idea almost exploded inside her. She'd quit working for Dud Dumars! If he called, she'd tell him that she didn't want another job, that she had decided to retire.

After all, she was over fifty. Yes! She would quit working for Dud! Then there wouldn't be the secret between her and Robert! She laughed under her breath at the simple solution. Now that she wouldn't have to think about taking a job if Dud called her, she could sing in the summer concert and she'd have plenty of time to practice for the wedding she was singing at next month.

Suddenly Heidi screamed, pushed Caro down hard, and grabbed for the plastic phone she held tight to her. "I had it first! Grandma, make her give it back!"

"Give it back, Caro. You can play with this." Carolynn rolled a large red and blue ball to Caro.

Caro dropped the phone and with a giggle pushed the ball across the room just as Stan walked in. He still lived at home in two rooms upstairs that he'd turned into his office and his bedroom. He wrote the popular "Skip Reagan Adventure Series" for boys and was a substitute teacher at the middle school in Middle Lake. This morning he looked like he'd been pulled through a knothole backwards. He hadn't shaved for two or three days and he wore a baggy, tattered gray sweat suit, which completely hid his muscular body. His dark hair was uncombed and he had a black smudge under his right eye.

Carolynn's heart swelled with love for him. He was her youngest, her baby. "Did you have breakfast, Stan?"

"I'm not hungry." He yawned. "Mom, I need a favor."

She smiled and rolled her eyes. "What?"

He knelt beside her chair and kissed her cheek. "Could you do a load of wash for me?"

"Stan! You promised when you moved back home that you'd take care of yourself."

"I know, but I have a deadline and I need some clean clothes. Just this once, mom."

"I did all your laundry last week and the week before."

He grinned and jumped up. "I know. Thanks. I promise this is the last time I'll ever ask you to help me."

Carolynn laughed and her blue eyes twinkled. "Tell me another one, Stan."

Caro tugged on the leg of Stan's sweat pants. He hoisted her high in his arms, then sat on the overstuffed chair beside the rocker and talked to Caro and Heidi.

Carolynn watched him, her eyes soft with love. "You need kids of your own, Stan."

"I need a wife first, mama."

"I know. I've prayed for her since you were a little boy."

"You told me." He watched the girls chase the ball across the floor.

"Have you seen Holly Loudan lately?"

Forcing back the flush that threatened to creep up his neck and over his face, Stan laughed. He knew his mother wanted to match him up with Holly. He and Holly had dated all through high school, but she'd married Ben Loudan shortly after. Ben had died suddenly two years ago from a tumor on the brain. Stan occasionally took Holly to dinner. At times he even thought of marrying her, but always pushed the frightening thought aside. "I think she's interested in someone else."

"Who?" Carolynn asked sharply. She really believed Stan and Holly belonged together.

"Paul Caine."

"He's not for her!"

Stan laughed. "As if you know, mom."

"Mother, women are marrying younger men these days, in case you haven't noticed."

Carolyn shrugged, then grinned. "I suppose it's only fair. Men have always married younger women."

Stan pushed himself up. "I do appreciate you doing the load of clothes for me, mom."

"You owe me one." Carolynn laughed. "One? You owe me a thousand!"

"I know, and I'll pay you back. I left the load in the laundry room." Stan kissed her cheek with a loud smack, walked to the hall, and up the open stairway.

Sighing heavily, Carolynn stood up. Were they doing Stan a great disservice by allowing him to stay home instead of getting his own place? An apartment cost so much, though, and Stan had worked hard since college to make it as a writer. If he'd had the extra expense of his own place he wouldn't have been able to write so many books. But he might've led a more normal life and even found a wife. "Who would do his laundry," said Carolynn with a laugh.

"Girls, let's go to the laundry room and start a load of clothes for your uncle Stan."

With the girls running ahead of her, Carolynn walked toward the laundry room off the kitchen. She hesitated at the basement door. Should she walk down and see Robert? She touched the doorknob, then pulled her hand away. It wouldn't do any good to walk downstairs. He wouldn't talk, and she couldn't tell him her secret with the little girls here.

Carolynn squared her shoulders and lifted her chin. "I won't take another case, so why tell him?"

Chapter 3

Raeleen Ost leaned heavily on her wooden cane as she walked slowly across the back yard to her goat pen. Her big blond-and-white collies flanked her. She'd had the dogs for six years. The bigger one was named Bob Barker, the other The Price Is Right. She called them Bob and Price. Today she was sorry she'd named them that.

She frowned at the dogs, then looked off across the wet grass to the wooden pen where her three nannies and one kid were kept. Maybe if she watched the kid awhile she'd feel better. The kid was a week old and already as smart as her mama. She was the only kid born this season, and just maybe Rae could keep her unless feed prices shot through the ceiling.

As she walked, Rae's long black coat swung around her skinny ankles. The coat was supposed to reach the top of her calf, but she was only five feet tall, so it hung longer. She wore black winter boots to keep her feet dry, an old white tee shirt of Ben's and blue bib overalls she'd bought in the boys' section at the clothing store at the grain elevator.

The rain had stopped, but the sky was still gray. Rain dripped from the small leaves on the maples. The oak, hickory and black walnut trees were as bare as during the winter. A goat bleated. Rae smelled the wood smoke curling up her brick chimney atop her old farmhouse.

Today the trip from the back door to the goat pen seemed long. Before she'd fallen and hurt her hip last year she could run to the pen, do the chores and run back. Her children hated for her to run, said she could fall and hurt herself bad, said she needed to slow down. Well, now she'd slowed down, and had been forced to use a cane. Maybe now they'd be happy.

Rae stopped at the wooden fence and leaned heavily against it. She felt out of breath, tired even, and the day wasn't half over. Bob and Price sank to the ground at her feet, one on either side of her in the same spots where they always laid while she watched the goats. It was as if they'd chosen their own spots and wouldn't think of changing.

Between the rails, Rae watched the two Nubians standing on the wooden table that she'd set out for them. They liked climbing and jumping. The table and boxes she'd set out for them kept them happy. She had the nannies stand on the table when she milked them. She stood behind them with her pail and milked them quickly and easily. It was better than bending over or squatting down, especially since she'd hurt her hip.

Rae saw the kid jump to the top of a low wooden box. Just like her mama, she had long drooping ears, short black and brown hair, and a Roman nose. The kid playfully leaped around, but Rae's mind drifted back to the "The Price Is Right" program that she'd just watched. The stupidity of the woman contestant from Georgia who overbid the Showcase still frustrated her. Any fool would know a trip to the Bahamas, dining room set with dishes, and a snowmobile couldn't be $18,000! The man contestant from Washington had underbid almost $10,000, but he'd won because of that scatter-brained woman who had overbid! Rae pursed her lips and scowled.

If she ever got to Hollywood, to "The Price Is Right," she'd be the big winner. Why, she could name the price of every prize within a couple of dollars. Except for artwork. Now that she was dumb about. But who'd guess that some of that idiotic-looking art was so expensive?

Bob and Price lifted their heads and whined, then stood up, facing the dirt road.

Just then a red pickup turned into her place and she touched her head and realized she hadn't put on her brown wig. Her thin, baby-fine, white hair was her greatest embarrassment. That stupid contestant had rattled her so much that she'd forgotten her wig! Slowly she walked across the yard to the gravel drive, with Bob and Price flanking her.

She frowned at the pickup, then realized her visitor was Robert Burgess and she relaxed. He'd love her if she had no hair. He was like a son, a brother, and a friend all rolled into one. Before her husband, Ben, had died, he and Robert had worked construction together.

Robert stopped in front of his pickup, crossed his arms over his broad chest, and waited for Rae. He hated to see her have to lean so heavy on the cane. He knew the collies wanted to run to greet him, but they stayed at Rae's side as Ben had trained them to do when they were pups. Robert smiled at Rae. "Nice day for ducks," he said.

She laughed and shook her head. "Sure is." She stopped beside him and the collies licked his hands, then dropped down beside Rae. "What brings you out?"

"I needed a ride in the country."

"Good day for it."

"How're the goats?" He always asked about the goats because he knew they were her love.

"Doing good. The kid grew."

"Going to sell her?"

"I might. Want to buy her?"

Robert laughed, showing his strong, white teeth. He looped his hands around his wide green suspenders. "Where could I keep a goat?"

"In your basement."

"Carolynn wouldn't like that a bit."

Rae laughed. "Neither would the goat."

"I brought you something."

Rae's dark eyes lit up. He was always doing something nice for her. While Ben was alive, Robert had helped him with repairs around the place. Now he helped her if she needed it. He'd even learned to milk the goats even though he didn't like the job. "What'd you bring?"

"Those bluebird houses I promised you last fall."

She laughed in delight. "I spotted a couple of bluebirds yesterday."

"You said you have some wooden fence posts?"

"Sure do. Back of the shed." She pointed to the dilapidated shed several feet from the big barn. Old rusted machinery cluttered the ground at both sides of the shed. Later, weeds would cover most of it, but now it lay exposed and naked in its old age.

"Posthole diggers still in the shed?"

"Yup."

From the back of the pickup Robert lifted out three bluebird houses which he'd made from rough sawed cedar. The tops could be unscrewed to clean out the nest. Bluebirds had two, sometimes three broods a season, and the nests had to be cleaned after each.

With Bob and Price following her, Rae walked beside Robert to the shed. She knew he walked slowly so she could keep up with him. He was the strong, silent type and she admired him for it. Her five children all took after Ben; they talked too much. Robert was about the age of her oldest son, Jake. Robert was more like her than any of her children. He could stand beside her without speaking, and just enjoy the surroundings. When they reached the shed she said, "Anything new with you, Robert?"

"Not a thing." He wanted to tell her how upset he was over what Carolynn had tried to tell him this morning, but he knew he couldn't talk about it without his voice breaking. When he was in more control he'd tell her and see what she thought it would be. She had more wisdom than any woman he'd met and filled the gap that his mother had left when she died a few years ago. But she was much more than a mother figure to him. She was a friend, a real friend.

If he wanted to be quiet around her, he could without her feeling left out. If he wanted to talk, she listened without constant interruptions. He opened the shed door that hung on rusted hinges and stepped inside the cluttered shed. Cobwebs hung from the bare rafters. Old tools were stacked in uneven heaps. He spotted the posthole digger against the wall with shovels and rakes beside it. The digger's long wooden handles were gray with age, but the steel head was free of rust or corrosion. Robert glanced back at Rae. "Anything new with you?"

Rae waited until Robert picked up the posthole digger and stepped back outdoors beside her. "Adam's oldest daughter just had a boy."

"That makes your third, no, your fourth great-grandchild."

"Yes." Rae leaned heavily on her cane. "I guess I'm getting old." She took a deep breath and looked up at Robert. "Leena wants me to move to town."

"She always does." Robert shut the shed door as far as it would close.

"She says she won't take no for an answer." Rae felt tears sting her eyes and she blinked them away. She wasn't about to start crying this late in life. She could count on one hand the times she had let anyone see her cry. "She wants me to sell out and move into one of them places made for old people."

Robert felt Rae's agitation, but he didn't look at her as they walked toward the spot where he'd dig the first posthole. He knew she didn't want him to know how upset she was. "You can talk her out of it again. After all, you're an adult."

Rae laughed as he knew she would. They talked often about how their children suddenly wanted to mother them once they reached a certain age, and neither of them liked it.

Bob and Price sank down at Rae's feet. She frowned at them, still upset over the stupid contestant from Georgia. "You dogs get!"

They jumped up and ran across the yard, playing together like two pups.

The handles of the digger felt rough against Robert's hand as he bit into the soft earth with the steel mouth, then dropped the dirt into a pile beside the beginning of a hole. He pushed the handles together, rammed the steel head into the hole, pulled the handles apart and lifted out a fresh shovel of dirt.

Rae studied the dirt as if it were filled with gold nuggets. "This time Leena says if I don't move on my own, she'll put me in one of them rest homes. She says it's not safe for me out here all alone." Rae frowned at her cane. "Especially since I can't get around like I once did."

Robert lifted out another bite of sandy soil, damp from the morning's rain. "Leena calls you every morning."

"I know. But she's going to visit her kids in Oregon and will be gone part of April and most of May."

"Don't they have phones in Oregon?"

Rae chuckled. "I asked her that same question."

"I'll check on you."

"I'll tell her that." Rae watched Robert take a deep bite into the earth with the digger, lift it out, and dump the dirt on the growing pile. "But she won't think it's enough. She thinks I could fall while I'm feeding or milking the goats and nobody would find me until it was too late."

Robert leaned on the wooden handles of the digger as he studied Rae. She'd lost weight and her skin hung loosely about her neck and face. Only her dark brown eyes looked younger than her years. "Rae, there has to be an answer. One that would satisfy both you and your kids."

"But what?"

"I saw this thing advertised on TV. Some kind of call system. I don't remember the name. You buy a system that's linked with a special operator. If you fall, you press a button on a necklace-type thing that you wear around your neck. The button activates something on the receiver and sends a call out to the special operator."

Rae's face lit up. "I know what you mean! I saw it on TV, too." Her shoulders sagged. "It'll probably cost an arm and a leg."

"Not as much as living in an old folks' home."

"You're sure right about that. And a whole lot nicer. I could stay home where I belong, and Leena will get off my back."

Robert laughed and nodded.

"Next time I see it advertised I'll get the phone number and give them a call." Rae slapped Robert on the arm. His flannel shirt felt soft to her touch. "You made my day, Robert."

He smiled. She always managed to cheer him up, too.

"Did you happen to watch 'The Price Is Right' today?"

"No."

"You're lucky! There was this dumb woman from Georgia who couldn't guess her way out of a paper bag."

Chapter 4

Holly Loudan jerked open the storm door and pounded on the red door. "It's me, Aunt Flower!" Holly called just in case this was one of days Flower wasn't answering her door. She hadn't answered the phone even though Holly had let it ring twenty times before she'd given up and decided she'd have to drive over from work, then take the paper to school for Noah. He had called from school in tears because he'd left his science report at Flower's. Holly wondered if third grade was too hard for him. Maybe she should've let him repeat first grade when she'd seen how Ben's death had affected him.

A dull pain stabbed Holly's heart. Would she ever get over his death? With a ragged sigh she knocked harder on the door, hurting her knuckles. Yesterday Aunt Flower had said she'd be home all day.

Impatiently, Holly pulled her long burgundy coat tighter around her slender body to keep the wind from whipping it against the budding bushes beside Aunt Flower's back door. Occasionally Flower locked herself away from everyone. She said she needed to be alone so she didn't self-destruct from listening to all the problems at the abuse center. "Aunt Flower! It's Holly!

Open the door! I have to get a paper Noah left yesterday and I have to be back at the office at two!"

Holly moved restlessly and frowned down at the brown welcome mat, spongy from this morning's rain. She couldn't afford to ruin her new black leather heels.

The neighbor's gray terrier yapped on the other side of the wooden privacy fence. Wind blew a faint smell of fried chicken to Holly and she realized she was hungry. She'd ask Flower for an apple and a chunk of cheddar cheese to eat as she drove back to work.

Wind ruffling her short brown hair, Holly frowned at her watch. She had to be back to work in twenty minutes! She'd have to use the hidden key even though Flower didn't want her to in case someone saw the hiding place.

Holly lifted the corner of the soggy mat, pulled back a special velcro tab and inched out the key. Flower loved designing ingenious secret places to hide things.

Holly slipped the key in the lock and it turned easily. She pushed the key back in place, dropped the corner of the damp mat and wiped her fingers off with a tissue from her coat pocket.

She opened the door and warm air rushed out along with an unpleasant odor. Holly wrinkled her nose. Flower's house usually smelled of apple and spice potpourri. The house seemed strangely quiet except for the ominous tick of the antique walnut grandfather clock near the front door.

"Aunt Flower?" whispered Holly. Why had she suddenly felt the need to whisper? Just then chills ran up and down her spine and she gripped her black purse tightly.

"She's not here," Holly muttered as she walked through the utility room and into the kitchen where Noah had said he'd left his paper.

Holly stopped short beside the kitchen table. Her heart leaped to her mouth and her dark eyes widened in terror as she stared down at a man lying in a pool of blood on Aunt Flower's usually spotless kitchen floor between the table and the butcherboard-topped island. A knife stuck out of his chest. It was Aunt Flower's special boning knife!

Holly swayed and caught herself against the table. A bitter taste filled her mouth and perspiration popped out on her forehead and upper lip. She couldn't take her eyes off the man.

Blood covered the front of his pink shirt and the side of his expensive-looking gray, burgundy and pink tie, and ran down on either side of his dark gray suit jacket.

Her hand over her mouth, Holly staggered back and collapsed into a ladder-back chair. She felt a scream building inside and she choked it back. She must not lose control!

Where was Aunt Flower?

Holly turned away from the terrible sight, cradling her arms against the pain in her heart. Maybe Aunt Flower was dead in her bedroom or hiding in her closet. Holly shook her head. No, her aunt would never cower.

"Aunt Flower?" whispered Holly. She had to get up! She had to see if Flower was there! Holly's legs trembled and her face turned as white as the refrigerator. She crept down the hall that led to the two bedrooms. What if the killer was lurking behind a door, waiting to stick a knife in her? She shivered and almost ran, but the thought of her precious aunt forced her on. She searched both small bedrooms, the bathroom and the living room, then forced herself to walk down to the basement. Aunt Flower was not there, nor was anyone else.

A minute later Holly leaned weakly against the door frame between the kitchen and the hall. Was this a nightmare because she was nervous about Paul Caine coming to dinner tonight to meet Noah and Paige?

Holly swallowed the bile in her mouth and started toward the hall that led to the connecting door of the garage. The phone rang and she jumped and clamped her hand over a shriek. She stared at the white phone until it stopped ringing abruptly in the middle of the fifth ring. Maybe she should've answered it. It could've been Aunt Flower. But Aunt Flower didn't know she was coming to get Noah's paper.

She had to call the police. She shook her head hard. Not the police! Not with Aunt Flower's special boning knife sticking in the man's chest. Suddenly Holly thought of Carolynn Burgess two houses down.

"Carolynn will help me," whispered Holly. "She'll know what to do." During her growing up years when Holly had visited Aunt Flower she'd played with Carolynn's children. She'd dated Stan Burgess during high school. She knew more about Carolynn Burgess than her own family knew. Yes, Carolynn would help.

Holly reached for the phone, then drew her hand back. She couldn't stay here with a dead man on the floor beside her! She'd get Carolynn and bring her here to see what should be done.

Outdoors, Holly's heels sank into the grass, bright green from April showers, as she cut across the neighbor's back yard. Her hand trembled as she rang Carolynn's back door bell. She knew her face was as gray as the clouds scudding across the sky and that her brown eyes were wide with terror, but she couldn't mask her fear.

Carolynn Burgess opened the door. She smiled and said in happy surprise as she ushered Holly inside, "Holly Loudon! It's wonderful to see you! Come in!"

Suddenly Carolynn narrowed her blue eyes. "What's wrong, Holly? Did something happen to Noah or Paige?" Carolynn knew in the back of Holly's mind was the fear of her children dying just as her husband, Ben, had.

"Oh, Carolynn!" cried Holly, bursting into tears and flinging her arms around Carolynn.

Carolynn gasped at how distraught Holly was, but held her tightly as she silently prayed for her. Carolynn was thankful that Caro was taking a nap and Heidi was watching TV in the den. Robert was in the basement, building birdhouses again. He'd left immediately after lunch, but had come back a minute ago. Stan had eaten lunch with them, then gone back upstairs to his office to work on his book.

"Holly, God is always with you to help you in any situation," Carolynn said against Holly's soft brown hair. "I'm here to listen and I'll be glad to pray with you and help in any way I can."

Holly dabbed at her eyes with a tissue and blew her nose. Her hands shook so badly that she could barely hold the tissue.

Carolynn's soft flannel shirt suddenly felt too warm. The short hairs on the back of her neck stood as she watched Holly try to compose herself. This was a worse situation than she'd first thought. Silently, she prayed for wisdom to help Holly.

Holly grabbed Carolynn's hand and held on tight. "I need you to — to go to Aunt Flower's with me. There's a — a dead man," whispered Holly, her eyes wide, round saucers in her ashen face.

Carolynn gasped and looked quickly around to make sure Robert hadn't come up from the basement. Holly had accidently learned about Carolynn's work as an investigator when she was a teenager dating Stan. She'd promised never to tell and to Carolynn's relief, she hadn't told anyone. "Dead, Holly?" Carolynn asked carefully, just above a whisper.

Holly nodded. "Blood! A knife in his chest. Aunt Flower's boning knife!" Holly shivered and a bitter taste rose in her mouth. "And Aunt Flower's gone!"

Carolynn wanted to grab her jacket and rush to Flower's with Holly, but she suddenly remembered her promise to herself. She would not get involved! Let the police handle it. "You must call the police, Holly."

"No!" Holly shook her head hard. "Please, please, Carolynn! I need you!"

"But I can't do anything."

"You can!"

Carolynn shook her head.

"But why?"

Carolynn saw the anguish on Holly's face. How could she turn Holly aside? Maybe she could just go to Flower's with Holly and check things out, then call the police from there. But she wouldn't do more than that! "I'll get Robert to watch Heidi and Caro."

Carolynn hated to ask Robert to watch the kids, because lately he'd been ornery about everything. She eased Holly down on a chair just inside the kitchen, squared her shoulders, took a deep breath, and opened the basement door in the hallway outside the kitchen. "Robert?"

"What?" He felt better after his time with Rae, but he didn't want to be forced to listen to Carolynn's confession!

Carolynn's stomach knotted. "I must go out for a while. Will you watch the kids?"

Robert flung down the dust cloth that he'd used to get the last of the sawdust off his wren house. "Get Stan to watch them. I'm leaving right now to deliver these houses." It was past time that Carolynn learned his birdhouses were important!

She knew it wouldn't do any good to argue with him. He wouldn't offer to deliver the birdhouses later nor would he offer to take the kids with him. She closed the basement door with a snap, then hurried back to Holly. She hadn't moved and Carolynn patted her arm. "I'll be another minute, Holly. Just hang in there, honey."

Holly nodded. It was much easier to let Carolynn deal with the terrible problem.

Carolynn pressed the intercom button next to the kitchen telephone. When Stan answered she said, "I need you to come here right now, Stan. It's urgent."

"Mom, I can't" he cried.

"You must, son. I'm sorry, but you must." She knew he was debating on coming down or not, but she'd never had to tell him that he *must* before. That would make him come just out of curiosity.

From the hall closet Carolynn grabbed her black purse and warm blue denim jacket and hurried back to the kitchen.

Stan ran down the stairs and into the kitchen. He wore the same baggy gray sweats, his dark hair was still uncombed and he hadn't yet shaved. He stopped short when he saw Holly and he quickly tried to rub his hair in place. His heart did the usual flip at the sight of her. She wasn't the most beautiful woman he knew, but she was attractive, with big brown eyes and pretty brown hair that he'd liked better before she'd had it cut short. "Hi, Holly. I didn't know you were here."

Holly looked down at her hands.

"How're the kids?"

"Fine," Holly managed to answer.

"Are you still seeing Paul Caine?"

Holly stared at him in surprise. "What?"

Stan flushed. He hadn't meant to ask that. "Sorry. I know it's none of my business." He suddenly felt like an awkward teenager instead of a grown man. He turned to his mother. "What's so urgent?"

Carolynn reached up and kissed Stan's jaw that was rough with whiskers. She couldn't let him guess what was going on. "Honey, I must run an errand with Holly, but I'll be back as soon as possible. Take Caro potty when she wakes up and don't let Heidi watch more than fifteen more minutes of TV. If I'm not back in time, give them a snack. I'm sure you can find something. Kate will pick them up no later than four."

"Four!" cried Stan. "Will you be gone that long?"

"I might be." Carolynn took Holly's arm. "Let's go."

"What is so important that it can't wait?" asked Stan, crossing his arms over his broad chest and glowering at them much like Robert would have done.

"We don't have time to talk about it now," said Carolynn as she ushered Holly outdoors. But she knew she wouldn't ever talk about it to her family.

Wind whipped against Carolynn and her sneakers sank down in the soft grass as they walked across Jessica Waldron's yard, then Tim Ayres's to Flower's house.

"Maybe she's home now," said Holly, her teeth chattering.

"I'll knock," said Carolynn. She knocked twice, then Holly slipped out the key and unlocked the door with an unsteady hand.

"Don't let Flower know you saw this," said Holly as she slipped the key back in place.

Carolynn was impressed with the hiding place. "Does anyone else know about it?" she asked.

"No. Only Flower and me."

Carolynn stored that bit of information away in her head and stepped inside with Holly right behind her. She wrinkled her nose at the smell of death as she strode to the kitchen.

Holly gasped and turned away from the body. "I hoped it was a nightmare," she said raggedly.

"I'll call the police for you," Carolynn offered.

Holly gripped Carolynn's arm. "No! Don't call! I'm so frightened!"

Carolynn patted Holly's icy hand. "I'll check things over." But then she'd call the police and hand over all the information she'd gathered to Sheriff Farley Cobb.

Steeling herself, Carolynn bent over the body to check all the details just as she'd done before when she'd investigated murder cases. She slipped on a glove and checked his inside jacket pocket. She pulled out a worn black leather wallet and flipped it open. "His name is Peter Chute and he's thirty-four years old," she said. "Know the name, Holly?"

"I don't think so."

"Think about it while I jot down some information off the credit cards." Carolynn pulled a worn, small, spiral notebook from her purse and quickly wrote down the card numbers and expiration dates of the three cards. She jotted down his description and the brand of suit he wore. She checked his other pockets and found in his right jacket pocket a scrap of paper with Flower's address on it — not her name, only her address. Carolynn frowned slightly as she slipped the paper back in his pocket.

In his left pocket she found a small bag of M & Ms, half empty. She looked around the floor and found a green M & M against the toe kick at the sink. "He was here long enough to eat some candy and put the bag back in his pocket," she said. That meant that he'd stood here in the kitchen and talked to Flower. "He's not a salesman. One would never eat in front of a customer."

Holly struggled to find her voice. "I've never seen the man before. I thought I knew all of Aunt Flower's friends. You know she doesn't let anyone in her house that she doesn't know!"

"I know." Carolynn narrowed her blue eyes in thought. "Very strange indeed." Carolynn had known eccentric Flower Graidal for more than twenty years.

With her glove on, Carolynn opened drawers and cupboards. "Everything is in its place." She saw the maple block that held six knives. They were all in place. "I don't see any special place for that knife." She jabbed her thumb at the boning knife stuck in Peter Chute.

"I know," said Holly in a strangled voice. "That's what scares me so much."

"What?"

"Aunt Flower had a special place made for that knife and I'm the only other person that knows about it."

Carolynn's stomach knotted. "And where is that place?"

Holly walked to the sink and opened the cupboard doors under it. "Right here," she whispered hoarsely, pointing behind the stile. "It's her special boning knife for chicken and fish. She keeps it razor-sharp and she's the only person who ever uses it."

Carolynn lifted her dark brows, then bent down and looked and felt against the back of the stile. Built right against the stile was a holder for the knife. "If you didn't know it was there you'd never find it," she muttered.

"That's right," said Holly as tears welled up in her eyes. "Only me and Aunt Flower knew."

Carolynn's heart sank at the implication. "So you think she killed Peter Chute?" asked Carolynn softly around the hard lump in her throat.

Holly burst into tears. "She couldn't kill anything or anybody!"

"Maybe she was pushed beyond her limits."

"Then where is she?"

"I don't know. Maybe that's what I should work on first." Carolynn bit back a gasp. She was not going to *work* on anything! Didn't her promise mean anything?

"Can you find Aunt Flower and talk to her?"

Carolynn was quiet for several seconds, then finally she nodded. Talking to Flower wasn't really working on the case.

"What about the dead man?" whispered Holly.

Carolynn glanced at the phone. "We'll have to call the police. But, Holly, you must not tell them that I'm going to get involved in the case. Promise me that. You can't tell anyone. Promise me, Holly."

"I promise," whispered Holly.

"Before I make the call I should check the house and the garage."

"I looked everywhere but the garage," said Holly.

"Let's look again." Carolynn strode down the hall to the bedrooms.

"This is Aunt Flower's," said Holly. The queen-sized oak bed, a nightstand on either side, the tall chest of drawers and an eight-foot dresser with a huge mirror almost filled the room. The bright yellow, blue, and pink flowered curtains at the two windows matched the bedspread. Six small decorator pillows lay at the head of the bed; two were solid pink, two blue, and two yellow. A heavy oak rocker sat in the far corner beside a round table with a lamp on it. A plush blue carpet covered the floor. The walls were painted a glossy white. An oak-framed photograph of Holly, Ben and their two children hung on the wall beside the chest.

While Holly sank to the rocker Carolynn looked inside drawers and the closet as quickly as possible. Nothing seemed strange or out of place.

"The other room is the spare room, the one I slept in when I'd stay here and the one my kids sleep in when they come," said Holly weakly as she led Carolynn down the hall.

Carolynn glanced around the spare room. It was decorated in shades of pink with a bright splash of red as an accent. The drawers and closet were empty. She lifted the bedspread and covers and found a wrinkled bottom sheet. "Did you or the kids sleep over lately?"

"No. Why?"

"Someone slept in this bed and didn't pull the bottom sheet tight."

Holly gasped. "Who could it have been?"

"We'll have to find out. We both know your aunt wouldn't make a bed and leave the fitted sheet wrinkled."

"She never would! Never!"

Carolynn looked closer at the pillow, then lifted off a long strand of light brown hair. "Well, well," she said as she carefully tucked it into a tiny plastic bag that she carried for just such things.

"Carolynn, I'm so thankful you're helping me!" cried Holly, close to tears again.

Carolynn slipped the plastic bag in her purse and slowly closed it. Deep inside she felt excitement building just as she had on each case she'd worked on. Maybe she should take this one last case, then quit. Yes! Yes, she'd take the case! But it would be her very last! The excitement raced through her blood, and her mind started sorting through all the information she'd discovered so far.

Her senses alert to every little detail, Carolynn checked the basement where Flower had her pottery wheel and shelves for her artwork, but didn't find anything unusual. Upstairs, Carolynn opened the connecting door from the utility room to the garage. Holly stayed close behind. Cool, closed-in air rushed out. Carolynn stepped down the two steps into the two-car garage. Two shelves lined the side of the garage and held only a few items for yard work. A small lawn mower stood in a corner. A blue BMW was parked in the left spot. The other one was empty.

"Whose car is that?" asked Holly with alarm as she stepped closer to Carolynn. "Aunt Flower drives a '76 red Corvette!"

"It probably belongs to Peter Chute," said Carolynn as she opened the car door with her gloved hand. She checked the glove compartment for proof of insurance and found that the car did indeed belong to the dead man. She jotted down the name of the insurance company, the names of the music cassettes in the glove compartment and a list of the other items: two pencils, an unopened bag of M & Ms, a business card from a company called Vital Call and a Michigan map. The floor was clean. The keys were not in the ignition nor on the seat. Carolynn couldn't find the keys anywhere. They hadn't been in Peter Chute's pockets either.

"I'm so scared," whispered Holly, shivering.

"Let God's peace rule your heart, Holly," said Carolynn softly, patting Holly's shoulder. "Your strength comes from God. You can't afford to fall apart now." She hugged Holly, then walked her back to the kitchen. "It's time to call the police."

"Oh, look at the time!" cried Holly. "I was supposed to take the paper to Noah and be back at work over an hour ago! I don't dare lose my job!"

"After I call the sheriff you can call the school and your boss," said Carolynn. "Tell them you have a family emergency." That was an understatement, thought Carolynn grimly as she walked to the phone to call Sheriff Farley Cobb.

Chapter 5

With Holly trembling at her side, Carolynn held Flower's red front door wide for Sheriff Farley Cobb and Deputy Kit Littlejohn. Farley was fifty-five years old with brown hair sprinkled with gray, hazel eyes, and he was only an inch taller than Carolynn. His brown uniform jacket fit snugly across his big stomach, but the pants hung loosely on his thin legs. Kit Littlejohn was twenty-eight years old, well over six feet tall and almost too thin to cast a shadow. He had high cheekbones, black hair which hung to his collar and narrow black eyes.

"In the kitchen," Carolynn said. As usual Farley didn't give her away. He'd known about her undercover work for years, but he kept her secret. They worked together when it was necessary. She respected him for his intelligence and for the way he got his job done. She knew he respected her for the results she always got. But he couldn't understand why she stayed in the background and never took credit for her outstanding work. She'd told him it was because of her family, but still he hadn't understood. She'd always put her family before her job. She'd never missed a parent/teacher conference, a band concert or a football game or tennis match. Her investigation was arranged around her children and her husband.

Now that the kids were raised with families of their own, except for Stan, she had more free time. Since Robert had retired it had been a little harder to keep her secret life from him, but he wouldn't have understood. In fact, he would've insisted she quit, and that's why she'd never been able to tell him. After this case she would retire, and Robert would never have to know.

Kit Littlejohn nodded to both Carolynn and Holly, then followed the sheriff across the living room.

Holly slipped her cold hand into Carolynn's. "I'm so afraid they're going to think Aunt Flower killed the man," she whispered.

"She *will* be a suspect," said Carolynn grimly.

"I'm so scared for her!" Holly gripped Carolynn's hand tighter. "You will stay here with me, won't you? Please?"

Carolynn wanted to get on with the job of finding Flower, but she could see Holly was in no shape to be alone. "I'll stay." She helped Holly off with her coat, pulled off her jacket and draped them both over a blue overstuffed armchair. Holly wore a medium-gray, light-weight wool skirt and a mustard-colored sweater.

"Let's sit down, shall we?" Carolynn could see Holly was close to collapsing as they sat side by side on the flowered sofa. A rocking chair sat across the coffee table from them, with a red, blue and white afghan draped over the arm. Flower had decorated according to her taste and not the current fashion. A long table of houseplants sat between two bookshelves full of books. An old upright piano stood against another wall.

Carolynn flipped open her small notebook and read the questions she'd jotted down: Who spent the night in Flower's guest room? Where is Flower? How is Peter Chute connected with Flower?

Her brow furrowed in thought, Carolynn slipped the notebook back in her purse.

Just then Farley poked his head around the doorway of the living room. In the background Kit was making phone calls to the ambulance service and the medical examiner. "Either of you know the deceased?" asked Farley.

"No," said Carolynn while Holly only shook her head.

"When do you expect your aunt home?" he asked Holly.

"I don't know," said Holly weakly.

"When did you arrive, Mrs. Loudan?" asked Farley in the gentle way he had of speaking. Carolynn knew the gentler he spoke the more he suspected the person. His tone worried her.

"A few minutes after one," said Holly, gripping her icy hands together in her lap. Her sweater suddenly felt too warm even though the room was cool.

"And how did you get in?"

Holly shot a look at Carolynn, then looked back at the sheriff. Would she have to tell him about the hiding place? Flower would hate that! "With the back door key."

"Then what?"

Carolynn studied Farley as he listened to Holly's account. From the look on his face and the way he stood with his notebook in hand, scribbling from time to time, she knew he was wondering if Holly had stabbed Peter Chute. Being suspicious was Farley's job, but he was being ridiculous if he thought Holly Loudan could kill anyone.

As Holly answered questions, the grandfather clock bonged four o'clock and Carolynn jumped. Stan would be ready to tear his hair out if Kate hadn't picked up Heidi and Caro by now. Well, Stan needed practice with kids. One of these days he'd decide to pull his nose out of his work long enough to find a wife. And if he looked close enough to home, he just might find Holly Loudan.

Finally Farley walked back to the kitchen and Holly sank against the couch with her eyes closed, her face ashen.

Carolynn pushed herself up and impatiently paced the room. She had to *do* something! She couldn't sit and wait!

She glanced out the window. Just then Flower stopped on the street in her '76 red Corvette. The police car and Holly's car filled the short space of the driveway. Carolynn's heart hammered as she shot a look toward the kitchen. She had to have time alone with Flower before Farley Cobb did!

"Holly," whispered Carolynn as she grabbed her purse and jacket. "I must go out for a while, but I'll be back." She couldn't tell Holly that Flower had driven up or she might do something to give it away to Farley.

"But where are you going?"

"Out! I can't wait. Explain to the sheriff that I had to leave, but that I'll be back." Carolynn eased out the front door and ran to the curb just as Flower was getting out of her car.

"Carolynn, why are the police here?" asked Flower in alarm. She wore bright pink, loose-fitting rayon pants and a jacket with a pink, red, and yellow blouse, and pink shoes with flat heels. Her dyed red hair hung to her slender shoulders. Her face was oblong and her skin smooth. She was very attractive and looked closer to forty than sixty. "Has something happened?"

Carolynn caught Flower's arm and tugged her toward her Corvette. "We must get away from here and talk!"

Flower ran around to the driver's side and slipped in as Carolynn slid in the passenger side. Without another word, Flower drove away from her house and turned the corner onto Maple Street and drove several blocks down the residential area to the main street of Middle Lake. She pulled into the empty back parking lot of the public library, parked, and turned to Carolynn. "Now, what's wrong?"

Carolynn saw the concern in Flower's brown eyes. As quickly as she could, Carolynn told Flower everything.

"Pete Chute dead?"

"Yes."

"My boning knife?" asked Flower hoarsely.

"Yes." Carolynn watched her closely.

"But no one knew where I kept it!"

"Not even your houseguest?"

"She didn't."

Carolynn's stomach tightened. "I told Holly that I'd help."

"But what can you do?"

Carolynn shrugged slightly. Flower didn't know the truth about her work. "I can find the person who stayed in your spare room."

"I don't understand." Flower brushed back her hair. Pink loop earrings dangled from her pierced ears. "Why does it matter? Why shouldn't I go home and tell all of this to the sheriff?"

"You should, but first I want to have a chance to speak to the person who stayed at your house."

Flower looked closer at Carolynn. "Do the police suspect her?"

Carolynn cleared her throat. "Actually, they suspect Holly. And you. They don't know about your houseguest yet."

Flower sagged against the seat, shaking her head in bewilderment. "I've never been involved in murder before."

"I don't suppose you know who killed Peter Chute?"

"I don't," whispered Flower. Suddenly she sat forward and gripped the steering wheel. "Mink said he'd left! She came out to meet me at the curb and said he'd left without hurting her."

Carolynn wanted to pull out her notebook and jot down the information she knew Flower would reveal, but she didn't dare to do so in front of Flower. "Suppose you tell me everything you know about Peter Chute."

"I don't know much at all." Flower fingered the top button of her bright blouse and narrowed her eyes. "I know he beats his wife."

"Oh?" Carolynn lifted her brow as she tucked her left leg up under her and turned to watch Flower as she talked. "Tell me about his wife."

"Mink Chute. Thirty years old. Quite attractive. But scared out of her wits. She came to the abuse center about a month ago and talked to me about her husband, Pete." Flower took a deep breath. "I told her to walk away from him, but she wouldn't. Then a few days ago she came again. Her left eye was swollen shut and she was bruised all over."

Flower's face hardened. "I wanted to force Mink to move into the home for battered wives, but she wouldn't do it. She said she wanted to give Pete another chance. Another chance!" Flower spit out the words, then took another deep breath. "He was always sorry after he lost control, always promised he wouldn't do it again."

"Do you think she killed him?"

"No! Oh, I don't know! I don't think she did." Flower leaned her forehead down on her hands as she gripped the black leather steering wheel.

"Where is she now?"

Flower lifted her pale face and groaned. "I took her to the airport to catch a flight home to her parents in Indianapolis."

Carolynn bit back a groan. She needed to speak with Mink Chute now. "How did Mink come to be at your place?"

"Last night about ten she stopped at the center just as I was ready to leave. Mentally she was a real mess! I broke all the rules by asking her to go to my house. But I couldn't get her to check in at the home! And she was desperate." Flower bit her lower lip.

"She ate dinner with me and talked nonstop. She said she was finally ready to get away from Pete. This morning while we were eating breakfast she said she wanted to talk to Pete one last time before she went to stay with her parents. I finally agreed to let Pete come to my place, so she phoned him. When he got there

I left them alone, took my clothes to the cleaners and paid a couple of bills. I gave them an hour, then drove back.

Pete's car was gone. Before I got out of my car, Mink ran to meet me. She said she was ready to leave, so I took her home to pack, then to the airport. I waited until her plane was ready to take off, and I left. Then I stopped at the abuse center awhile." Flower sighed heavily. "I had no idea Pete was dead on my floor."

"If Mink didn't kill him, who did?"

Flower spread her slender hands and shrugged.

"I must talk with her, Flower."

Flower dug in her pink leather purse. "I have her parents' address and phone number in here somewhere." Finally she pulled out an old Comsumer's Power bill envelope with scribbling on the back and handed it to Carolynn. "Here it is. Her parents live outside of Indianapolis, so she said she wouldn't get there until after five."

"I'll give her a call," said Carolynn, tucking the envelope in her black purse. "Did you talk with Pete at all?"

"Just to say hello. He was eager to be alone with Mink."

"Was he eating M & M's?"

Flower frowned at the strange question. "No. He seemed too upset to do anything but settle the problem with Mink. He did not want her to leave him. He seemed to really care." Flower hit the steering wheel hard with her palm. "Why wouldn't he get help? It makes me so frustrated!"

"He's past help now," said Carolynn as she put both feet on the floor. "We'd better get back. Sheriff Cobb will want to talk with you." Carolynn was silent a moment. "It would be better if you didn't mention that I waylaid you. He might be upset about that."

"Should I tell him about Mink?"

"Yes. Yes, tell him everything."

Flower started the car and gripped the gear shift, but didn't move. "Carolynn, no one could accidently find my boning knife. I made sure of that."

A chill ran down Carolynn's spine. Would Flower in her anger and frustration kill Pete Chute? "Did you use it and leave it out while Mink was there?"

"Of course not! It's been over a week since I used it."

Carolynn stared down the long red hood of the Corvette. She hated what she was thinking.

Several minutes later Carolynn followed Flower into her house.

"Aunt Flower!" whispered Holly, flinging her arms around Flower.

Flower held Holly close. "It'll all be sorted out soon."

Sheriff Farley Cobb walked into the living room and cleared his throat as he frowned at Carolynn.

Carolynn lifted her chin a fraction. "Sheriff Cobb, Flower Graidal."

"I need to ask you a couple of things, Mrs. Graidal," said Farley.

Frowning, Holly stepped back from Flower. "She didn't kill that man, sheriff! She couldn't kill anyone!"

Nodding, Farley smiled slightly. "I never said she did." He motioned for Flower to have a seat. "Suppose you tell me about Peter Chute and how he came to be here."

Carolynn stepped forward. "Farley, could I interrupt a moment?"

"Sure," he said, shrugging, but he didn't close his notebook or lower his pencil stub.

"If it's all right, I'd like to leave."

"That's fine," said the sheriff.

"Take Holly with you," said Flower.

"But I want to stay with you!"

Flower patted Holly's arm. "You go with Carolynn. I'll be all right. I'll call you at home later."

"Are you sure you don't need me here?"

"I'm fine." Flower looked at the sheriff. "Aren't I?"

He nodded. "Nothing but questions."

Carolynn gripped Holly's hand and pulled her up. "Call me too, Flower."

"I will."

"I will too," said Farley, his eyes narrowed.

Carolynn smiled and walked outdoors with Holly. "I'll drive, Holly. I'll leave you at my place."

"I could go home."

"No. You don't want the kids to see you this upset. Stay with Stan. He'll take care of you." Carolynn parked the car in her driveway. "You go in the front door and

I'll go in the back. I don't want Stan or Robert to know I'm home yet."

A minute later Carolynn slipped into her bedroom and closed the door. She had a few calls to make in private.

At the front door Holly trembled as she rang the door bell.

Stan Burgess opened the door, then stepped aside and let Holly walk in. He closed the door and looked at her bent head and drooping shoulders. Her mustard-colored sweater was spotted with tears and her eye makeup was smudged. Stan was alone in the house. Kate had picked Caro and Heidi up right at four and his dad was still gone. Stan had shaved and changed into dark-blue dress pants and a white dress shirt just in case Holly came back with his mother. "Where's mom?" asked Stan.

"She said to wait here for her." Holly swayed and would have fallen, but Stan caught her and steadied her.

"Hey, what's happening here, Holly?" Stan wanted to pull her close and hold her tight, but he eased her down on the couch and sat beside her. He saw the pallor of her face and felt her tremble. "Talk to me, Holly."

She took a deep, steadying breath. "I might as well tell you. It'll be on the news tonight."

Stan whistled softly. "It's a little worse than I thought, it seems."

Holly shuddered. "A man named Peter Chute was murdered at Aunt Flower's house earlier today. I...I found...the body."

"Oh, Holly!" Stan pulled her close and she clung to him. He smelled the light scent of her perfume, closed his eyes and rested his cheek against her soft hair. She fit in his arms as if she'd been made for him, and he thought of the times his mom had suggested he let Holly know how he felt about her.

Silently he prayed for Holly, and even for himself to have the courage to sort out his feelings for her, then talk to her about them.

Finally Holly pulled away, but kept her hand nestled in his, and in a ragged voice told Stan about Peter Chute. She stopped herself just in time before she told him about Carolynn's promised help. "The police actually suspect me and Aunt Flower! Not enough that they arrested us."

"But how can they suspect either of you?"

She told him about the boning knife. "Aunt Flower and I are the only ones who know where it's kept."

"Maybe she used it and left it out."

"Never! When she uses it, she immediately washes it and puts it away. You know Aunt Flower."

Stan nodded. He liked her, but he'd always thought she was weird. "If there's anything I can do to help, I will."

"Thanks. But there's nothing."

"I can pray."

Holly nodded. "Yes. Yes, do that!"

"This'll be pretty hard on Noah and Paige."

Suddenly Holly jumped up. "Oh, I hadn't realized how late it is! My babysitter will want to leave. I must get home!"

"I'll take you."

"But I have my car here."

"You're in no condition to drive across town. I'll get your car to you later. Dad'll help me." Stan slipped on his jacket and walked her to the garage. A few minutes later he backed his four-door, medium-blue Ford out of the garage and drove down 10th Street to Ash, turned on 2nd Street and later onto Linden Street. He glanced at Holly to see that she had her head back and her eyes closed. She looked suddenly too frail to handle Noah and Paige on her own. "I'll take the kids out to McDonalds and give you a chance to rest."

"Thank you," she whispered as a tear slipped from under her long lashes and rolled down her cheek.

Love for her rose inside him until it almost overwhelmed him. Or maybe it was sympathy. He frowned as he slowed for a stop sign. Why was he so afraid to love Holly? Maybe he thought she'd reject him again as she had done just after high school. He'd asked her to marry him, but she'd refused. With a broken heart he'd gone away to college and when he'd seen her again she was engaged to Ben Loudan.

Stan pulled into the drive at 1215 Linden and looked at the ranch-style home where Holly and Ben had lived most of their married life. Now Ben was gone and Holly lived alone with nine-year-old Noah and ten-year-old Paige. Stan taught Noah in Sunday school, so he saw him every Sunday. Noah was quiet, too quiet, Stan thought. Paige made up for it. She was like a noisy butterfly, always flitting from one thing to another.

Stan shut off the car, but sat still, his hand gripping the steering wheel. If he opened his heart to Holly again would another man walk right into Holly's heart? Maybe Paul Caine?

Abruptly, Stan pushed aside his thoughts and helped Holly out of the car.

"Oh, no!" she cried.

"What?"

"I just remember Paul Caine is coming to dinner tonight to meet the kids!"

Stan's jaw tightened. "You're in no condition to cook dinner."

"I know." Holly drooped beside him and he slipped a steadying arm around her waist. "Stan, would you call him and ask him to make it another night?"

Stan's stomach knotted at the rotten thought of talking to Paul Caine. "Sure, I'll do it, Holly."

"You're a good friend, Stan."

Friend? Is that all he was to her? His face set, Stan walked Holly to her door. He didn't want to call Paul Caine, but he could see Holly was in no shape to do so. And if he didn't call, Paul would show up on her doorstep, expecting dinner and a fun evening with Noah and Paige.

Several minutes later Stan stood alone in the kitchen, the white receiver to his ear. On the fifth ring Paul answered. Stan wanted to crush the receiver into powder.

"I have a message from Holly Loudan."

"Who is this?"

"A friend of hers." A muscle tightened in Stan's jaw. "Stan Burgess."

"How are you, Stan?"

"Fine."

"How come Holly's not calling?

"She's had a rough day." Stan heard Holly talking with Noah and Paige in the living room. "She has to cancel dinner with you."

Paul was silent for a long time. "Tell her I'm coming anyway."

Stan stiffened. "She says she doesn't want you to come. She's very upset."

"Are you staying?"

"For a while."

"Then I'll be there shortly."

Anger shot through Stan. "I won't let you in!"

"Since when do you have a say in Holly's house or in her life?"

"Since now." Stan slammed down the receiver, his face red and his hands knotted into fists. This time he would not step aside! This time he'd stand his ground! Paul had better not stop by!

Slowly Stan walked to the living room to be with Holly and her kids. It was past time for him to face his feelings for Holly and to learn just how she felt about him.

Chapter 6

Friday morning Carolynn slipped in the back door of Dud Dumar's office so the others in the outer office wouldn't see her. Dud had three detectives working for him as well as the secretary, Mable Greene. Mable wouldn't allow anyone in to see Dud or the detectives unless they had an appointment. Carolynn didn't have an appointment.

Dud sat behind his large steel desk, a Tony Hillerman mystery in his hands. He peeked over the top of the book with a look of surprise in his hazel eyes. Sunlight from the window behind him bounced off his bald head. He wore a white shirt open at the neck and dark gray dress slacks. "You ever read this?"

"No."

"It's good." Dud stuck a yellow pencil in as a marker and dropped the book on his cluttered desk. The room was small, but not crowded. A black, fake leather couch sat against the wall opposite the desk. An antique trunk sat in front of the couch as the coffee table. A steel folding chair stood near the desk. "How's Robert?"

"Working on birdhouses."

"A pair of bluebirds are nesting in the house he put up for us."

"That's nice."

"Sometimes I wonder if I wouldn't be better off building birdhouses. Meg would be happier."

"Maybe not."

"Oh?"

"We don't talk like we should, Dud. The communication between Robert and me is at an all-time low."

"Birdhouses don't have a thing to do with that!"

Carolynn sighed heavily. "I know."

"So, did I call you?"

"No." Carolynn sat on the straight-back chair across the desk from Dud. She crossed her legs and rubbed her hand over her black dress slacks. Her black leather shoes with flat heels gleamed from the polishing she'd given them last night when she couldn't sleep. She'd called Mink's parents and learned from her mother that Mink had not come home, nor was she expected to. She had said she was happily married to Pete Chute and lived in Middle Lake, Michigan. Carolynn hadn't told them differently. They'd learn soon enough that Peter Chute had been stabbed with a razor-sharp boning knife. Just why had Mink let Flower believe she was going to Indianapolis?

Carolynn moved restlessly. The chair was uncomfortable, but Dud wanted it that way. He said it kept clients from taking too long to tell him what they wanted. Carolynn fingered the top button of her flowered rayon blouse. It was tucked in at the waist of her black linen slacks with an emerald-green linen jacket over it.

"You here to shoot the breeze?"

"I wish."

Dud cocked his bushy white brows. "So?"

"I'm working on the Peter Chute murder."

"Ah! I saw it on the eleven o'clock news last night."

"It's a puzzle, Dud."

"I didn't hire you."

"Nobody did. I'm helping out a friend. Holly Loudan."

"And her aunt Flower Graidal?"

"Yes, but Flower doesn't know it."

"You and your *secret identity!*" Dud laughed as he leaned forward. "So, what'd you want from me?"

"I need information on Peter Chute." Carolynn dropped the page of data and questions about Chute beside Dud's veined hand.

Dud nodded, lifted his phone receiver, pressed a button and said, "Mable, give me a printout on Peter Chute." He rattled off the information and the questions from the paper, dropped the receiver in place and held the paper out to Carolynn. She slipped it back in her purse. "So, you could've done that over the phone."

Carolynn dropped both feet flat on the floor and leaned forward, her elbows on her knees. "It looks a lot like either Flower or Holly killed Chute."

Dud whistled long and low.

"Looks like, Dud! I know differently. Now, I have to prove it." But what if she was wrong? What if one of them *had* killed Chute? The thought was too terrible to consider. She told him about the boning knife and the special hiding place for it.

"Do you want me to put one of my people on it?"

"No. I want you."

"Me?"

"You're the best."

Dud shook his head. "Can't help you, Carolynn. I'm taking Meg on a long-awaited trip. Leave tomorrow."

Carolynn sighed heavily. "Can I talk you into postponing a day or two?"

"No. I promised Meg, and this time I won't break my word." Dud tugged at the open collar of his white shirt. "She's had to put trips aside time after time, Carolynn, and I promised her that she wouldn't have to this year."

Dud leaned back and studied Carolynn thoughtfully. "You can handle this one on your own."

"I've never been so personally involved before, Dud. These are women I know. I don't want them to be guilty. If they are, I don't want to be the one to send them to prison."

"I hear you, Carolynn. I guess you have to put on your professional facade, and work twice as hard and twice as fast to prove your friends didn't kill Chute. You better see who else had a motive."

"Motive might be simple. Opportunity is quite another matter."

"Just who built that special holder?" asked Dud.

Carolynn shot from her seat as if she'd been stung. "Someone built it! Not Flower, I'm sure. She's good with her hands, but I don't think she could make the wooden holder and mount it so carefully on the stile. Why didn't I think of that?"

"It took this," said Dud, grinning as he tapped his head with his finger. "Little gray cells, as Hercule Poirot would say."

Carolynn couldn't laugh, not even at Dud's immitation of the famous Belgian from the Agatha Christie novels. "I can't do this one on my own, Dud!"

"Aren't you the gal that's always telling me you're never alone? Got the Lord on your side?"

Carolynn grinned sheepishly and nodded.

The phone buzzed and Dud picked it up, listened, then said, "I'll be right out to get it." He knew Carolynn didn't want the others to know she was there.

She stepped to the side of the door as Dud walked out; he returned with a paper in his hand. Then he closed the door and held the paper out to her. Quickly she scanned it.

"He had a good credit rating. Worked for a business called Life, Inc. for the past two weeks, before that he worked as an ambulance driver for eight years. Had a wife, Mink. No children." Carolynn shook her head, her brows knit together. "No police record, not even a parking ticket." She rolled the paper and tapped it on her palm. "How could a man suddenly have enough money to drive a BMW and dress in $500 suits?"

"Win the lottery?"

"He didn't."

"This is America."

"Sure, I know."

"Land of opportunity."

"I think I'll pay a visit to the office of Life, Inc., and see what I see," said Carolynn.

"What about his wife?"

"She had motive and opportunity."

"But?"

"She didn't know where the boning knife was kept. She couldn't have done it."

"There's always a slight chance of coincidence. Maybe she was under the sink for something and ran across the hiding place."

"Maybe." But Carolynn doubted it. "She was supposed to go to her parents, but she didn't go. I checked her place. She wasn't there. Maybe she did kill him, then flew off somewhere, never to be found again."

"That'd make it hard on your friends."

"You're right." Carolynn started for the door. "Have a nice vacation, Dud. Tell Meg I'm thinking of her."

"Before you go, I'd like to ask a favor." Dud leaned back on his desk and crossed his skinny ankles. His dark gray slacks hung loosely on his thin frame.

Carolynn walked back toward him, her brow cocked.

"I want to tell Jay Sommers about you."

"Your newest detective?"

"Yes."

"But why?"

"So he can call on you for help while I'm gone. He's good, Carolynn. Young. Twenty-five. But sharp. He has more natural ability for this business than either Christine or Albert. If you and Jay teamed up you'd solve every case that came our way."

Carolynn cleared her throat. "Dud, I'd better tell you what I decided yesterday."

"Am I going to hate it?"

"Yes."

Dud walked around and sat down as if he'd suddenly grown very tired. "Tell me. Make it quick! I don't have all day, you know."

Carolynn sank to her chair again and gripped her purse on her knees. "This is the last case I'm going to take. The last!"

Dud burst out laughing and slapped his leg. "Carolynn, you had me scared there for a minute."

"I'm serious, Dud."

"Sure. Quit. Like you can stop breathing."

"I won't argue, Dud, but I am serious. I have to work on my marriage. Giving up the business will be my start."

"Is that what Robert says?"

"No." Carolynn wrinkled her nose and grinned. "I didn't tell him."

"So, tell him! Let him in on your decision. Who knows? He might decide to join you in solving crimes. He's got a keen mind."

"He'd never want to snoop around!"

"Ask him. You might be surprised."

She shook her head. "I can't even imagine it, Dud. This is my last case. It is!"

Dud rubbed a thin hand over his bald head. "If you need help while I'm gone, you talk to Jay Sommers. I'll jot him a note."

"That's not necessary."

Dud pulled out a yellow legal pad and scribbled several lines, folded the page and stuffed it in an envelope, which he addressed to Jay Sommers, then leaned across his desk and held it out to Carolynn. "Put it in your purse. If you don't need it, fine. But if you do, it's there. It'll make me feel better since Meg and I will be gone for over a month."

Reluctantly Carolynn pushed the envelope into her purse next to the printout on Pete Chute. "Thanks, Dud. You and Meg have a wonderful vacation!" Carolynn didn't get up. She could see Dud had something more to say.

"We will. I promised her." Dud rubbed his hand over his bald head. "I sure miss having her work here with me."

"Maybe she'll be up to coming back after your vacation."

"Maybe." Dud looked ready to cry. "Maybe."

"Is there something you're not telling me, Dud?"

He forced a grin. "We're not spring chickens, Carolynn."

"What's going on here, Dud?"

"You're the detective."

Hot tears stung Carolynn's eyes as she thought of Meg's decline in health. "I'll be praying for you both."

"You do that." Dud walked slowly around his desk and reached for Carolynn's hands. He squeezed them hard, then turned away, but not before she saw tears sparkling in his hazel eyes.

She wanted more information about Meg, but she could see he wouldn't say more until he could get his emotions under control. Silently Carolynn prayed for Meg, then for Dud. "I'll stop in when you get back."

"You do that."

Without another word to Dud, Carolynn slipped out the back door. She hated to leave him when he was feeling upset, but she knew he'd want her to. Inside her car she pulled out her notebook and wrote: Who built the special knife holder for Flower, and when? Carolynn flipped to the very last page of the notebook which was marked "Prayer List." She added Meg Dumars to it, closed it, then flipped it back open and wrote "Dud" under Meg's name.

Several minutes later Carolynn parked in the only empty space outside the building that held the office of Life, Inc. Cars of every description and model lined the street to the end of the block. She studied the five-story brick building that had once been a department store which had gone belly up because of the mall just outside of town. Now it was full of offices. A greasy-spoon joint, the Bluebird Cafe, stood to the left of the building and Clem's Barber Shop to the right. Sunlight sparkled off one puddle that still remained from yesterday's rain. Smells of coffee, hamburgers, and car exhaust hung in the air.

Carolynn walked into the foyer of the building, read the list of offices on the freshly painted wall. Life, Inc. was on the first floor behind a solid wooden door with LIFE INC. in bold, block letters on it. She stepped inside, onto a thick beige carpet. A black woman in her mid-thirties sat behind a walnut desk with a leather pad built into the top of it. A white phone with buttons enough for three phones sat on the desk beside a memo pad and calendar. Canned semi-classical music played softly. Three brown leather chairs sat against a wall to the left of the door. Above them hung a large water color of bright wild flowers, a clump of birch trees and a pond with a white, cast-iron bench beside it. It was one of the most beautiful paintings Carolynn had ever seen. Finally she looked back to the woman to see her smiling at her.

"Beautiful, isn't it?" said the woman. Her make-up enhanced the beauty of her ebony skin and black eyes. She wore a white suit with a red, white and black scarf. A name plate on her desk read Floy Tedmund.

"I love flowers!" said Carolynn as she stepped closer to the desk.

"Can I help you with something?"

Carolynn glanced past Floy Tedmund to a hallway with offices lining it. "Peter Chute."

Floy Tedmund's smile froze. "What about Mr. Chute?"

"May I see him?"

"I'm sorry, but he's not in."

Didn't Floy Tedmund know Chute was dead? Or was she keeping the information from the customers? "I want to make an appointment."

"How about with Mr. Moran? He has a few free minutes."

Carolynn sighed and put on a disappointed look. "I really wanted to see Mr. Chute."

Floy Tedmund rested her hand on the phone. Several diamond rings sparkled on her slender hands. Her long nails were painted bright red. "Mr. Moran can explain Vital Call to you just as well."

"If you're sure."

Floy Tedmund smiled. "I'll buzz him."

"Wait!" Carolynn held out her hand and the woman frowned. "I've changed my mind." Carolynn made a point of looking at the brass nameplate. "Ms. Tedmund. I should've brought my husband with me. He usually handles this kind of thing."

"Does one of your parents need Vital Call?"

"My mother. But I think it might be better to get her a nurse instead."

Ms. Tedmund shrugged slightly as she folded her hands in front of her on the desk. Her sleeve moved, showing a gold watch circled with diamonds. "Do as you like, but Vital Call does give elderly people the opportunity to stay home like they want."

Carolynn moved one step closer to the desk. She smelled Floy Tedmund's expensive perfume. Carolynn clutched her purse in front of her. "I've heard about Vital Call, but could you explain again how it works?"

Ms. Tedmund walked slowly around the desk and stopped beside Carolynn. "Mr. Moran could explain much better than I can."

"I really do feel more comfortable with you." Carolynn didn't want to meet Mr. Moran quite yet.

Ms. Tedmund tucked her fingertips into the pockets of her figure-hugging jacket. "The recipient wears the button on a chain around her neck. If she falls or has trouble breathing, she pushes the button, which activates the system on the phone. It rings in to our special operator and she calls back, then if necessary she calls an ambulance, the family, the police, or whoever needs to be contacted. Within minutes, help is on the way. It's a wonderful method of protecting the person who really shouldn't live alone, yet insists on it."

In the back of her mind Carolynn remembered hearing about someone she knew who had used Vital Call. Who was it? Well, she wouldn't push at her memory or she'd never remember. If she left it alone, the information would surface and she'd have it. Yes, she'd leave it alone and before long she'd remember.

She smiled at Floy Tedmund. "I do think Vital Call would work for mother, but I must check with my husband. I'll give you a call. But I will want to speak to Mr. Chute."

"I should've told you sooner." Floy Tedmund looked uncomfortable. "Mr. Chute is no longer with us. He...died suddenly yesterday."

Carolynn pressed her hand to her throat and widened her eyes. "Oh, I'm sorry to hear that! I'm sure you're upset about it."

"Yes, I am. He was a friend as well as a business associate."

"Did you work together long?"

"Since the company came here."

"Did he leave a family?"

"A wife. No children."

"I can imagine how hard it is on his wife to make the funeral arrangements and all."

"Yes. Yes, I'm sure it is."

"I know I could never handle something like that on my own! Does she have someone to help her?"

"I suggested a funeral parlor to her this morning."

"Was it Kribbs?"

"Yes. Why?"

"I've heard they take very careful care of the grieving loved ones. Not like at Ashton's! They charge much too much. I heard they steal the jewelry from the bodies in the coffins. Right out of the coffins! No, don't have her go to Ashton's!"

"She won't. She's going to Kribbs." Floy Tedmund walked back around her desk. "I am very busy today, Mrs.... I didn't get your name."

"Jane Withy." Carolynn had used that name many times before and it fell off her tongue as easily as her own name. She turned toward the door. "I'll talk with my husband and be in touch.'

"Your phone number, Mrs. Withy?"

"I'll call you, Ms. Tedmund." Carolynn opened the door and walked out before Floy Tedmund could ask anything else. Carolynn shot a look at her watch. It was noon. This might be a good time to drop in at Kribbs' Funeral Home and see if Mink Chute was there. "I have some questions for her," said Carolynn grimly.

Chapter 7

Outdoors, just off the wide front porch, Bob and Price barked sharply, and Raeleen Ost knew a car had turned into her driveway even though it wasn't twelve yet. She'd changed from her chore clothes into a pair of black slacks and a pink sweater, her daughter Milly had given her for Christmas, and she wore her brown wig. She'd even put on a little lipstick and a dusting of powder.

With a frown, she tugged aside the lacy white curtain and looked out the living room window just behind her chair. The living room was a square room with a door on each wall except for the wall with the windows that looked out onto the driveway. She sat in her favorite rocker with Ben's blue chair beside it, a matching blue couch on the wall to her left and the TV on the wall to her right.

"The Price Is Right" was still on TV and she'd specifically told those folks at Life, Inc. not to come until noon when it was over. It was time for the Showcase and today both the contestants were smart. One of them just might come within $100 of the price and win both showcases. If Life, Inc. thought she'd miss that, they'd better think twice!

A dark blue Lincoln Contintental stopped near the lilac bush and Rae knew the folks from Life, Inc. would try to use her front door. When she'd talked to them on the phone yesterday and set up the appointment, she'd told them it wouldn't do any good to knock on the front door. It was blocked shut with a wardrobe and had been for fifteen years. Maybe getting the special device from Life, Inc. wasn't a good idea after all. If they were this stupid about simple directions, how could she trust their Vital Call thing-a-ma-jig? Just maybe she'd let them knock on her front door until their knuckles turned black and blue and the game show was over.

Bob and Price barked harder and Rae knew someone had gotten out of the Lincoln Continental. She craned her neck until she could see a mustached man in his thirties dressed in a medium gray suit, white shirt and red and gray tie, and a black woman dressed like she'd just stepped out of a catalog walk toward the front porch. Rae had told them she wouldn't deal with a man alone, so they'd promised a woman would accompany the salesman. At least they'd remembered that part of the deal. The collies barked at the couple's heels, making them walk a little faster.

The commercial was over and Bob Barker made a wisecrack about the contestants, then announced that the Showcase would begin.

Rae let the curtain fall back in place and sat on the edge of her rocker, her eyes glued to the color TV screen. Ben had bought the 25-inch set for her a few years ago when she told him she was tired of watching their 13-inch screen. He'd almost bought a VCR to go with it, but hadn't done so because he couldn't figure out how to work it and Rae knew she couldn't either.

Just then someone knocked on the front door. Scowling, Rae glanced toward the hall door, then quickly back at the television. The top winner passed the first Showcase to the runner-up. Rae leaned forward. "$12,500," she said. The woman bid $12,500, and Rae beamed with pride.

Someone knocked again and Rae was sure it was the man from the sound of the loud rap. If he was dumb enough to knock on her front door, he could knock 'til the cows came home, but she wouldn't answer.

Rae watched the second Showcase and almost jumped out of her seat at the fabulous trip to Scotland.

She'd always wanted to go there. So had Ben. They never had the money, but they had big dreams. The last prize they showed was a pickup that looked a lot like Robert's. "$20,000," said Rae in a tense voice. She wanted the young redhead from Wisconsin to win. She bid $19,800 and Rae said, "That's fine. You should win."

The man knocked harder just as the commercial started. Rae leaned heavily on her cane, walked slowly to the hall, and shouted, "Use the back door!" Under her breath she muttered, "Dummy. Can't follow simple directions!" She walked back to the living room and stood about three feet from the TV. Outdoors Bob and Price were barking wildly. Rae knew they wondered why she didn't come to the door. She always did when they barked. They ought to know she was watching TV and couldn't answer the door yet.

The man knocked on the back door just as Bob Barker announced both correct prices. Both women were within a few hundred dollars of being right, but the big winner was the redhead from Wisconsin and Rae grinned. "Almost won 'em both," she said as she clicked off the TV. "If I'd been there, I'd have won 'em both."

The man knocked again, this time harder.

"I'm coming!" shouted Rae as she gripped her cane. "Keep your britches on, will you?" She chuckled under her breath. She ought to keep them waiting even longer just to teach them to follow instructions.

She walked through the dining room (which she never used unless the children came for dinner), into the kitchen, and to the back door. Bob and Price were in a real frenzy. Rae opened the door and the collies immediately stopped barking and sank to their haunches in the back lawn.

"Raeleen Ost?" asked the man, a smile on his good-looking face, but anger in his dark eyes. His mustache twitched and he switched his black briefcase from one hand to the other.

"Yes." Rae nodded, but didn't step aside for them to enter. She wanted to know for certain they were from Life, Inc. before she let them cross her threshhold. A woman alone couldn't be too careful.

"I'm Linus Moran and this is Floy Tedmund. We've come to talk to you about Vital Call."

"It's a pleasure to meet you face to face after speaking to you on the phone," said Floy, her pink bracelets jangling as she moved her hand. She wore a pale pink linen suit with a hot pink silk blouse and matching pink earrings. Her purse and shoes were the same shade of pink as her suit.

"I *was* expecting you, wasn't I?" cried Rae in mock surprise. Inside she laughed at her own joke, then chuckled drily as she stepped aside. "I thought you'd wait until after twelve."

"I thought it was after," said Linus Moran, motioning for Floy to step in ahead of him.

Rae looked at the large wooden kitchen clock. It was two minutes after twelve. "So it is," she said. She peered out the door. Robert had promised to come listen to the sales pitch. She knew he'd never come until after twelve. He never bothered her while she was watching "The Price Is Right." She wished she could say the same for her family and for these two from Life, Inc.

"I understand your family wants you to move to town, but you want to stay here on your own," said Moran.

Rae nodded, looked back outdoors, then finally closed the door. The refrigerator hummed softly and the floor creaked. The kitchen was big and cheery, with yellow counters and curtains and oak cupboards. The linoleum floor needed to be scrubbed, but she'd not felt up to it, so she'd left it dirty.

"So, you're interested in Vital Call," said Linus Moran.

"Yes." Rae leaned heavily on the cane as she walked to the oblong yellow formica table with four matching chairs. "We can sit right here to talk about it." She'd cleaned the kitchen extra well this morning, but still the counters were cluttered and one kitchen chair held a stack of newspapers. Rae sat down in the chair nearest the back door and leaned her cane against the table.

His briefcase in hand, Linus Moran sat on one side of Rae, and Floy Tedmund sat on the other side. Rae smelled Moran's aftershave and Floy's perfume. (Rae preferred the smell of goats and dogs.)

"Mrs. Ost," said Moran in his salesman voice.

"Call me Rae. Everybody does."

"Rae. I'm Linus and this is Floy."

Rae nodded and smiled and knew she'd forget their names before five minutes had passed. Just then Bob and Price barked.

"Robert's here," she said, slowly standing. Her knees cracked and she flushed. She hated for people to know her bones were old. "I told him to come listen to what you have to say about this thing you want me to buy."

"Is Robert your son?" asked Floy with a tight smile, her slender hands folded in her lap.

"No. Friend." At the sound of his step, Rae opened the door and Robert smiled. He wore a white dress shirt and navy blue slacks. He looked very business-like. "Come on in, Robert. Move them newspapers and sit there."

Robert held out his hand to Moran. "Robert Burgess."

Moran shook hands. "Linus Moran. This is my associate, Floy Tedmund."

"Glad to meet you," said Robert, shaking Floy's hand. He dropped the newspapers beside the refrigerator and sat down. "Have you told Rae about the system yet?"

"Just getting ready to," said Moran as he clicked open his briefcase. He pulled out several papers as well as a necklace-like thing with a red plastic button on it. Together he and Floy talked about Vital Call.

Rae listened, feeling more excited as they talked. This indeed was the answer to her problem! With Vital Call installed she could stay home without her children always on her about moving into town. She smiled at Robert and she could see he was impressed also. The price was higher than she'd wanted to pay, but she had the money. Right now she'd spend almost any amount of money to get to stay at her own place with her goats and her collies.

"Have you ever had a system malfunction?" asked Robert.

"Never," said Moran.

"Will it work if Rae is outdoors?" asked Robert.

"Yes," said Floy. "It's been tested to cover up to a quarter of a mile."

"I'll take it," said Rae. "When can you install it?" It would feel funny to wear the silly necklace all the time, but she'd get used to it. Now, she could relax, her family could relax, and everything would be all right.

*   *   *

Carolynn sat at a corner table across from Flower. The tables and chairs were made of pine, and ruffled blue gingham curtains covered the front windows. Country paintings hung on the walls. It was too late for lunch customers and too early for dinner customers so they had the restaurant almost to themselves. Carolynn had planned it that way when she'd called Flower to meet her after she'd left Life, Inc. and the funeral home. Carolynn sucked on her chocolate shake, enjoying the cold, smooth drink. Country Home made the best shakes in all of Middle Lake.

Carolynn watched Flower calmly sip her hot honey water. Flower didn't seem to mind that she had to stay at a motel until the police unsealed her house. She didn't act flustered like others had in such a situation. Holly had offered to let her stay with her, but Flower had said she needed time alone. Carolynn dabbed her mouth with a white paper napkin. "I called Mink Chute's parents last night."

Flower lifted a red brow. "Did you speak with Mink?"

"She wasn't there." Carolynn told Flower what Mink's mother had said. "Are you sure Mink stayed on the plane?"

Flower slowly set her cup down and nodded. "I know there wasn't time for her to get off. It was taxiing out when I left. I suppose it could've been called back."

"It wasn't." Carolynn had checked that. "Her mother could've been lying to cover for her."

"That's true. Maybe Mink did kill her husband." Flower fingered her multi-colored hoop earrings as she frowned in thought, then pushed back her shoulder-length red hair. "But if she did, I can't imagine how she found the knife. Unless it wasn't as hidden away as I'd like to believe."

Carolynn rubbed a hand over the sleeve of her green jacket, then fingered the top button of her flowered blouse. For once she was dressed in brighter colors than Flower who wore a high-necked, big-sleeved gray dress with a yellow scarf and bright earrings. "Flower, who built your knife holder for you?"

"Flet did. About three years ago."

Carolynn filed the information away in her mind to jot down later in her notebook. Fletcher Raabe lived in the colonial house just behind Flower. Something nudged the back of Carolynn's brain, then was gone. She didn't try to force it out or she'd lose it altogether. "Is Flet home from his son's yet?"

"Not that I know."

Carolynn wanted to talk to Flet. "I heard he was thinking of selling his place."

"He said he'd wait until he got back to decide." Flower leaned forward, her brown eyes troubled. "Sheriff Cobb asked me to stay around. He said I can't leave town. Does that mean he seriously thinks I could've killed Pete Chute?"

Carolynn didn't want to answer that question. "What motive does he think you have?"

Flower leaned back with a sigh. "He knows how upset I was because Mink wouldn't leave Pete."

An icy knot tightened in Carolynn's stomach. Just how upset had Flower been? Enough to commit murder?

Flower folded her white paper napkin several times. "I'm not allowed to work at the abuse center until my name is cleared."

"I'm sorry."

"Me too. It's a hard place to work, but it's important to me." Flower moistened her red lips. "My dad beat my mom. I couldn't do anything as a kid, but I vowed I'd do something when I grew up. I can't tolerate filling my days with fluff while folks out there need help!"

Carolynn hadn't known about Flower's parents. Carolynn glanced at two chattering women walking to a table nearby, then she turned back to Flower. "Did the sheriff say he was going to check on your alibi?"

"He didn't say."

"He probably will, you know."

Flower shrugged. "Let him. I was telling the truth."

Carolynn felt ashamed that she'd even doubted Flower. Of course she was telling the truth! But a tiny doubt remained and Carolynn knew she'd have to check Flower's alibi just to make sure she wasn't allowing her feelings to get in the way of the case. On any other case she'd check every alibi of every person involved.

Just then Carolynn saw a man and woman about her age walk into the restaurant. The man had his arm around the woman and was talking with his head bent close to her ear. She smiled and blushed. Carolynn bit the inside of her lower lip. It had been a long time since she and Robert had gone out together. It had been even longer since he'd whispered something to her that made her blush. Would they ever get back the romance they'd shared in the past? With effort, she pulled her mind off Robert and back to Flower.

Flower sipped her honey water, then carefully set the cup down. "I told Holly I want to hire a private investigator."

Carolynn stiffened.

"She said I should talk to you first. I said it wasn't necessary, but she made me promise. She got very agitated and wouldn't calm down until I finally agreed. So, I'm telling you my plans."

Carolynn locked her hands in her lap. "Who did you have in mind?"

"Dumars Investigative Services. I found them in the yellow pages."

Carolynn's mind raced. "And when will you speak with them?"

"I have an appointment in a few minutes.'"

Carolynn's heart sank. This was one of those times when she wished others knew abut her work. Suddenly she thought of Jay Sommers, the young man Dud had wanted her to contact. Maybe she could work something out after all. "I've heard about one of the men working there. Jay Sommers. You could ask for him."

Flower brushed her hair back. "Actually, I already decided to work with their only woman investigator, Christine Lavery. I'd feel more comfortable."

Carolynn bit back a moan. Lavery, as she wanted to be called, was not one of Carolynn's favorite people. Dud only kept her on because Meg liked her. Carolynn could tell Flower had made up her mind, so she only shrugged and said, "Are you sure you shouldn't leave the investigation up to the police?" Farley had said that to her a million times, and she'd always disagreed. It didn't surprise her when Flower did. "I take it Holly doesn't want you to hire a detective."

"She doesn't see any reason to. But, of course there is. She doesn't realize just how close we are to being arrested. And I didn't have the heart to tell her."

"I'd think the sheriff would be out looking for Mink Chute," said Carolynn, watching Flower for a reaction.

"I don't think he believes she was at my house. He acts like I made it all up."

Carolynn knew Farley felt that way. She'd talked to him just minutes before meeting Flower. Farley had laughed at the clues she'd uncovered; the wrinkled bottom sheet on the spare bed and the long, light-brown hair.

Farley had said, "I know Flower and Holly are friends of yours, Carolynn, but I'm going to have to arrest Flower Graidal. She had opportunity and motive. A wrinkled sheet and a hair won't help here."

"Give me a little more time, Farley."

He'd sighed and finally had said, "One more day. That's all. If I don't see new evidence by five tomorrow afternoon I'll arrest Flower Graidal."

Farley's words rang in Carolynn's ear as she watched Flower prepare to leave. "Flower, I'll do everything I can to help you!"

"I know, Carolynn. But what can you do? I appreciate your friendship and your love, but this takes a professional." Flower picked up the check and held it high as Carolynn reached for it. "I must hurry to make my appointment with Christine Lavery. I'll talk to you later."

Carolynn nodded. "And next time I'll pay!"

Flower grinned, shrugged, and walked to the check-out counter.

Carolynn slowly stood, then watched the man and woman across the room, envious of their relationship. Finally she walked outdoors to her car. She had more to do than watch a couple making calf eyes at each other! She had to find out why Floy Tedmund had lied to her about Mink making funeral arrangements for Peter Chute. His body hadn't been released by the coroner yet. The funeral director at Kribbs hadn't heard of Mink or Peter Chute. So, why had Floy Tedmund lied? And where was Mink Chute?

★   ★   ★

Stan leaned his elbow out his open car window and rested his head on his hand while he watched the door of Jackson Realty and Construction, a nice office building that had once been a filling station. The small parking lot was half empty already. The noise of traffic on the freeway a block away sounded louder than usual. Holly had told him she got off at 4:30. It was 4:35 and still no sign of her. Several others had walked out right on the dot of 4:30. Holly hadn't been one of them.

Stan tugged at the collar of his white shirt and ran his fingers through his dark brown hair he'd had cut today because he'd wanted it to look nice when he picked up Holly. Last night he'd listened to her as she told over and over about finding Chute's body. She couldn't seem to let it go. He'd stayed with her until she assured him that she'd be fine and that she would be able to sleep.

She was so afraid Flower would be arrested. Maybe she had a valid reason for being afraid. It sounded like she was the only person who could've killed Chute.

Stan frowned. Flower was weird, but she was soft-hearted and usually gentle. She couldn't stab another human.

Finally Holly walked out of the office. She wore a blue, light-weight wool skirt and a short-sleeved peach sweater. Paul Caine walked beside her, his arm draped around her shoulders, his face serious as he talked to her.

Jealousy shot through Stan like he'd never experienced before. He wanted to tear Paul's arm out of the socket. Had Holly forgotten that he was picking her up? She'd wanted to stay home, but couldn't afford to take another day off, so he'd driven her to work so she wouldn't have to contend with traffic or try to keep her mind on driving.

Holly said something to Paul and he smiled. For a minute Stan thought Paul was going to kiss her, but she moved slightly. On purpose? Stan couldn't tell.

Stan considered driving away, then he squared his jaw and opened the car door. "Holly," he called.

She looked up and smiled, glad to see him. She tried to pull away from Paul, but he tightened his hold on her.

"I'm taking her home, Burgess," said Paul gruffly.

Stan reached for his keys, but stopped himself. No, he would not give up so easily this time! He slipped from under the steering wheel and stood beside his car. "Holly?"

She didn't know what to do and she was too tired to decide.

Stan saw her hesitation and it tore at his gut. But it was hesitation, not rejection. He walked toward her, smiling at her. "We have a date, remember?"

She nodded, relieved to have the decision made for her. "See you tomorrow, Paul." She pulled away from him and this time he let her go. She saw the anger in his eyes, but she was too weary to bother with it.

Stan held out his hand and she slipped hers in his. His pulse leaped and he wanted to pull her tightly to his heart. Instead, he opened the passenger door, then closed it after her. He ran around to the driver's side and slipped in. The faint aroma of her perfume teased his nostrils. "We're going to stop for a pizza to take home. I tossed a salad and it's in the refrigerator. You won't have to cook or clean up."

She had her eyes closed and her head back against the seat. For the first time today she felt as if she could relax. "Thank you, Stan."

"My pleasure." He drove away from the parking lot and over to Baker Street for the pizza.

"Has your mother come up with anything new?" asked Holly.

"My mother?"

Holly sat up with a sharp gasp. She'd almost given Carolynn's secret away! "I mean, did any of you hear anything new on the case?"

"No. It was still big news on the twelve o'clock news, of course. And I'm sure it will be again at six."

Holly groaned.

"Something will happen to push it into yesterday's forgotten story."

"It can't be soon enough for me!" Holly leaned back with a sigh. "It's all such a nightmare!"

"I know. Just remember that God is always with you. *Always!*"

"I couldn't make it if He wasn't." Holly reached over to touch Stan's hand. "I'm thankful for you, too, Stan."

He looked down at her small, lightly tanned hand on his large, sun-browned hand. Could she hear his heart? Did she know the effect she had on him? If she did maybe she'd tell him to get lost. Fear trickled down his spine, but he reminded himself that God was always with him, even in this situation, and finally the fear disappeared. He smiled into her eyes and said softly, "What do you want on your pizza?"

Chapter 8

Her hands tucked under her head, Carolynn stared up at the ceiling, the light from the bathroom bright enough to show all of the bedroom except the far corners. She and Robert had repapered the bedroom only last year. The soft pastel flowers pleased her, and made her feel as if she had a special garden all year long. In the dimness she couldn't make out the flowers, nor the light yellow of the woodwork. She heard Robert brush his teeth and do all the last-minute things he did before he came to bed. What would he do if she sprang on him her involvement with the Peter Chute case? She bit back a sigh. She was too tired even to think about his anger.

Finally he clicked off the bathroom light and fumbled his way across the bedroom to the bed. He usually stubbed his toe on the quilt rack, but tonight he didn't. He slipped between the sheets and tugged the soft cover up over his shoulders. "Good night," he said softly.

"Good night," she said around the lump in her throat. The king-sized bed suddenly felt a mile wide. With their smaller bed they'd slept close together no matter how they felt, but now it took an effort to move across the bed to cuddle, especially if she didn't know if he'd freeze her out. Finally she said, "How'd your day go?"

"As usual." He wanted to tell her about Rae getting Vital Call, but he didn't think she'd be interested.

Carolynn heard a faint sound of music coming from Stan's room. He'd come home a few minutes ago, but had gone right upstairs. "I spent some time with Flower today."

"We always assume murder happens to people we don't know."

She didn't make that assumption, but she didn't say anything. "Flower hired Christine Lavery from Dumars to help her."

"That's nice."

Carolynn's jaw tightened. It wasn't nice! But then she couldn't say that either. Just what could they talk about that was safe? "The kids are all coming to dinner Sunday."

"Good." Robert liked it when they were all together. He heard the house creak as it cooled off. "It's been awhile."

"It has. For once they could all make it on the same day. I wanted them all here for Easter, but we settled on this Sunday instead. I think I'll make a turkey. Ham is just too salty."

"Make that special chocolate cake with the thick white frosting, will you?"

Carolynn smiled. "I didn't know you liked it."

"I do."

"Then I'll make it."

Robert wanted to slip over to Carolynn, but he stayed in his place in case she might push him away. Why couldn't it be the way it used to be when they'd both reach for each other at the same time? A great sadness settled over Robert and silently he prayed, "Heavenly Father, show me what I can do to bring us back together."

A great loneliness swept over Carolynn and she felt her nose tingle and her eyes burn and she blinked fast to stop the tears. This was ridiculous! She wasn't going to cry! But the tears welled up in her eyes and spilled over to run down the sides of her face. She used the sheet to catch the tears before they ran into her ears.

"I love you, Carolynn," whispered Robert, practically holding his breath for her response.

"You do?" she said, her voice breaking.

He stiffened. "Are you crying?"

"It doesn't matter."

"Why are you crying?"

She was quiet a long time. "I miss you so much!"

"But I'm right here."

"Only in body. You always seem so far away. Our spirits don't touch like they used to."

He groaned and slid over to her and pulled her tight to him. He knew what she said was true, but he didn't know what to do about it.

She turned in his arms and buried her face against his bare chest. Had the secrets she'd kept from him all these years done this to their marriage? Why hadn't she realized it? But maybe she'd wanted her life with Dumars more than she'd wanted Robert. The thought made her cling tighter to him to try to make up for her past.

Saturday, just after breakfast dishes were washed and put away, Carolynn walked outdoors for her usual morning walk, twice around the block at a fast clip. Robert was already gone for the day to help Wes and Kate with repairs they were doing on their house. Stan was at Holly's. Carolynn smiled, pleased that Stan was finally taking more time with Holly.

Piano music drifted out of the Gonzalas home as Carolynn walked past. The sun was bright, a promise that spring really had come to Michigan. But she knew it might not be a true promise. Year before last it had snowed in April and she'd worn her winter coat to church on Easter Sunday. But this morning she didn't even have to wear a sweater, only her jeans and her favorite black tee-shirt.

She slowed her pace as she grew closer to Fletcher Raabe's big white colonial house. A curtain moved behind an upstairs window. Flet was home. This would be a good time to drop in and have a chat about Flower's boning knife holder.

Carolynn ran lightly up the four wide front porch steps to the solid wood door. Later in the summer she knew the lattice work around the porch would be covered with ivy and a few climbing yellow roses. Marj had loved growing flowers as much as Carolynn did.

She pushed the doorbell and heard the chimes echo inside the large hallway. Marj had inherited the house from her parents.

Suddenly a memory clicked into place and Carolynn gasped, her hand over her mouth and her blue eyes wide. Marj Raabe had had Vital Call installed in her home! While Flet was gone, Marj had died all alone on her kitchen floor.

Peter Chute had worked for Life, Inc., the company that sold Vital Call.

Fletcher Raabe had made the special holder for the boning knife for Flower Graidal.

Was there a connection?

Carolynn took a deep breath and composed herself just as the door opened. Fletcher Raabe was well over six-feet-tall, lean with a balding head, hazel eyes full of pain and a gray stubble from not shaving in several days. He wore dark trousers that hung on his thin hips and a gray sweat shirt that had seen better days. "Morning, Flet," said Carolynn with a smile.

"I'm busy, Carolynn," he said in his deep voice. "I almost didn't answer the door, but I thought it might be the paperboy wanting his pay."

"I hadn't realized you were back from your son's."

"I didn't go."

That surprised her. "You mean you've been here all this time and didn't let any of us know? Oh, Flet, I would've brought a casserole to you, or something."

"No matter, Carolynn. I don't feel much like eating these days."

"I'm sorry, Flet."

He rubbed an unsteady hand over his stubble.

Carolynn glanced toward the white rockers on the porch to the right of the front door. "Would you mind if I sat down? I've been out for a walk."

Flet waved a heavily veined hand toward the chairs, then slowly walked with Carolynn and sat beside her.

Carolynn rocked gently for a minute, the creak almost comforting. She didn't want to appear as if she'd come to interrogate him. She stopped the rocker and turned her head toward Flet. "It's a shame that Marj was all alone when she died," said Carolynn, careful to keep her voice level.

Flet gripped the wooden arms of his rocker. "I never would've left her if I'd known that system didn't work!"

"But I thought Life, Inc. proved it was functioning properly."

"They lied! When I got home I tried it, and I got only the operator!"

Carolynn forced back her guilty feeling for having to play such a part with a friend. "I guess it was their word against yours."

Flet nodded. "But I'm right! Marj would be alive today if she could've gotten help. The thing didn't work!" Flet pulled a white hanky from his back pocket; he rubbed his eyes and blew his nose noisily.

"I never did hear the whole story," said Carolynn. "I'd like to, if you want to tell it."

Flet moved restlessly. "You don't want to hear it."

"Well, if you don't want to tell it — ." Carolynn let her voice trail off. She didn't want to appear too interested. She could see he wanted to talk about it, but was hesitant. "I know it still hurts a lot."

"Hurts!" Flet gripped the arms of his chair again and his face turned purple with anger. The words poured out of him as he told about Pete Chute coming to the house to tell them all about Vital Call. The company had their own ambulance service, paramedics, and an operator standing by at all times. It sounded like a good thing to both of them, so they had it installed.

Marj was glad to know help was at her fingertips. It made it possible for him to feel free to go to the grocery store and do other errands. He told about leaving on overnight business, but he didn't mention what it was. "When I got home I found Marj dead! I pushed that button myself to call for help. The special operator answered, but no ambulance rushed to our aid like they promised. Finally I dialed 911 and got someone right away. But it was too late for Marj. She was — dead."

Flet couldn't speak for a while and Carolynn sat quietly waiting. Finally he said he'd called Life, Inc. and they'd sent Pete Chute right over to check out the system. It had worked; the special operator answered and would've sent an ambulance, but Chute told them it wasn't necessary. Flet looked at Carolynn with bloodshot eyes. "Dead!"

The rage in his voice alarmed Carolynn. "When did you last see Chute?"

"How should I know?"

"You heard he's dead, didn't you?"

"I heard," said Flet grimly.

"Is anyone investigating Life, Inc. to see if it's legitimate?"

"I tried to get someone to, but nobody would."

"So, did you do it on your own?"

"I tried, but I didn't learn anything. But I know what I know!"

"I could ask around."

"You, Carolynn?"

"Sure. Who would suspect me of anything?" Carolynn grinned and Flet nodded without smiling. "I'd like to know myself if Life, Inc. is on the up and up. If it's not, I'd like it closed down."

"They can't stay in business. I'll see to that." Flet pushed himself up. "I got work to do. Can't sit around shooting the breeze all day."

"Do you think there've been other deaths because of Vital Call?"

"I don't know. Marj's death is what concerns me."

Carolynn walked toward the steps, then turned back just as Flet opened his front door. "Flet, there's a chance Flower will be arrested for Chute's murder."

Flet's arm jerked and he sagged weakly against the door. "Where'd you hear that?"

"Around."

"I thought they suspected Chute's wife. She was there at Flower's place with him."

Carolynn's heart thudded hard against her rib cage. Did Flet know what he was saying? Since he could put Mink on the spot, the sheriff wouldn't arrest Flower! Kit Littlejohn had questioned the entire neighborhood and no one had seen Pete or Mink Chute at Flower's house. "I think you should tell Deputy Littlejohn that you saw the Chutes at Flower's. Nobody believes her when she said Mink was there."

"I saw the deputy come to my door, but I didn't want to talk to him, not after the sheriff's department wouldn't do anything about Marj's death."

"Now they're going to arrest Flower for something she didn't do."

Flet rubbed his jaw and frowned in thought. "I'll tell the sheriff, but why didn't anybody else tell about seeing them?"

"Maybe nobody but you saw them."

"Or maybe they don't want to get involved."

"That could be too." Carolynn took a step toward Flet. "I wonder how Mink found the knife she stabbed her husband with."

"Maybe it was on the counter. Flower would know."

Carolynn nodded and her heart sank. It still came back to the knife. Mink couldn't be guilty. But Flet could. The knowledge hit Carolynn hard. She didn't want to believe Flet killed anyone. Or maybe Mink had accidently found the knife. Oh, what a merry-go-round! "Flower says you built the holder. Do you think Mink could find it on her own?"

Flet shrugged. "She could've."

"She's disappeared, you know."

Flet shook his head. "I didn't know. Ask them folks at Life, Inc. They know her. They know where she is."

"How do you know that?"

"She's in it with them. She was here with Chute when he gave us the sales pitch on the system."

That was a new wrinkle. Maybe Mink wasn't in Indianapolis, but was still here in Middle Lake with Floy Tedmund. Perhaps Mink had found the knife through a strange quirk of coincidence and maybe she had killed Chute. Carolynn watched a robin land on the lawn, then fly away as a boy on a bike rode by. She should look into Life, Inc. and see if it was legitimate. If it wasn't, there were a lot of helpless people in danger. She turned back to Flet. "Tell Sheriff Cobb about seeing Mink and Pete Chute at Flower's, will you?"

Flet hesitated, then nodded. "I'll call him right now."

"He'll want to see you in person, you know."

Flet frowned. "I don't know about that. I'm not up to going to the station."

"Have him come here instead. That wouldn't be so bad, would it?"

"I guess not."

"I'll talk to you later, Flet." She walked down the steps, then when she reached the sidewalk, turned and looked up at him. "I'm making a pot roast for dinner tonight. I'll bring you some."

He shook his head. "Couldn't eat it, Carolynn. I lost my appetite when Marj died."

"I'll bring some anyway. Eat it if you can." She smiled, lifted her hand in a wave and walked back toward home. Her walk was finished for the day. She had things to do and people to see.

Chapter 9

Carolynn took a deep breath and dialed Life, Inc. from her kitchen extension. After a lot of thought she'd decided she'd use Peg Graham's house. She was away for a month and had left the key with Carolynn to water the plants and feed the fish. It would be a perfect place for Jane Withy's old mother, Lola Windess. Carolynn rolled her eyes. She should've been a writer. She'd had to create enough characters down through the years to fill several books.

On the second ring Floy Tedmund answered in a pleasant voice.

"This is Lola Windess," said Carolynn in the old woman's voice she'd created several years ago. She'd used it many times already. "Jane Withy's mother. She told me about her visit to your office."

"Yes, Mrs. Windess."

"I want to see that thing she told me about." Carolynn shouted into the phone, "I won't move into one of them old folks housing places! I mean it!"

"And you shouldn't have to," said Floy. "We can certainly help you."

"I have this morning free for you to come, talk to me and show me the thing. Eleven-thirty."

"That would be fine. Our representative, Linus Moran, will be the man who will visit you. What is your phone number, please?"

For just a second Carolynn couldn't remember Peg Graham's phone number, then it popped into her head and she rattled it off. She gave the address and all the other information Floy Tedmund asked for.

"Linus will be there at 11:30," said Floy. "Thank you for calling Life, Inc., Mrs. Windess."

Carolynn hung up, then quickly dialed the sheriff at his home. "I know it's Saturday, Farley, but this is important."

"I'm sure it is," he said drily. She didn't have to tell him who it was; he knew her voice well.

Quickly she told him what Flet had said. "He'll be calling you. Please be patient with him." She explained how Flet was feeling about the Chutes, his wife's death and Vital Call. "Have you had any complaints about Vital Call, Farley?"

"If we've had them, they haven't reached my desk."

"I'm going to snoop around a bit." She didn't tell him she'd already set the wheels in motion.

"That's not a good idea, Carolynn."

"I have to, Farley."

He sighed heavily. They'd had this argument before.

"With this new information you won't arrest Flower, will you?"

"I'll listen to it, then see. Maybe Fletcher Raabe is a good friend who hates to see Flower go to jail."

"He is a friend. But he wasn't lying about the Chutes. I could tell." Carolynn twisted the white phone cord around her finger and watched a rabbit hop across the grass. "If I were you I'd find Mink Chute and see what she knows. Maybe she's your murderer."

"I wasn't going to tell you this."

"What?" Carolynn didn't like the tone of his voice.

"I talked to Mink Chute about an hour ago."

"No! In person?"

"On the phone. She said she'd just learned that her husband was murdered and she wanted to meet with me. She's been on vacation in Hawaii and will be home sometime tomorrow."

Carolynn sank to a kitchen chair, her legs suddenly too weak to hold her. "What's going on here, Farley?"

"That's what I'd like to know. Mink Chute says she's been in Hawaii for over a week. How could she have been at Flower's, killing her husband?"

"Then who was at Flower's?"

"My guess is nobody. She made it all up. Fletcher Raabe is only trying to help out a friend."

"I can't believe that, Farley Cobb!"

Just then the back door opened and Carolynn whispered into the receiver, "I have to go." She hung up, then stepped away from the phone just as Robert walked in. He smiled at her and she smiled back. Did she look guilty? He pulled her close and kissed her. She liked the fresh-air smell about him.

"I thought I'd come to take you out for lunch," he said with his arms still around her.

She stiffened.

Robert felt her hesitation and he drew back from her and let his hands fall to his sides. "Don't you want to go?"

"Of course I do! It's just that I was thinking of everything I have to do."

"The house is clean and you already know what you're making for dinner tomorrow. You said you didn't have to practice your song for the wedding until later today."

She touched his cheek and smiled. "But I do have to go take care of Peg's place." She saw the light in his eyes fade as he drew away from her until her hand fell. "I'm sorry, Robert."

"Sure. Yah. Me, too." He walked to the basement door, hesitated a moment, then opened the door and walked down to his birdhouses.

Carolynn sighed heavily. Maybe she should call Life, Inc. and cancel. "I can't," she whispered, then ran to get her special make-up case with the gray wig. She'd wear the brown slacks and baggy, tan sweater that she'd bought special as a disguise along with the wire-frame glasses.

With a tired sigh, Holly sat down beside Stan on the picnic bench at the park. She wore jeans and a white tee-shirt with three big yellow sunflowers on the front of it. The sun felt warm and the park was crowded even thought it was only ten-thirty. "I wish Aunt Flower would've come with us. It's not like her to want so much time alone."

Stan thought about taking Holly's hand in his, but couldn't get up the courage. "I thought you said she was meeting with that detective she hired."

"She did, and then the detective flew to Indianapolis to find Mink Chute." Holly had tried to call Carolynn to tell her that bit of news, but there'd not been a time when she was without the kids or Stan since she'd called Flower at nine this morning.

"Just relax and enjoy the day," said Stan. When he'd planned the picnic for Holly and the kids, he'd hoped it would take her mind off her problems for a while. It wasn't working, it seemed. He watched Noah and Paige playing soccer with other kids in the park.

"Thank you, Stan."

He turned to her with his brow lifted. "For what?"

She spread her hands wide. "For being here for me."

"Any time." He tensed. Was he ready for a lifetime commitment?

"I don't want to get used to having you around if you're planning to crawl back into your books once my problem is solved."

That hurt, and he couldn't speak for a while. "Is that what I do?"

She nodded slightly.

"Holly, I'll always be a writer."

"I know. And I think that's wonderful. But I also know you have a tendency to pull away from people who get too close. I don't want that to happen." Her lip quivered and her eyes filled with tears. "Don't take time for us because you feel sorry for me."

"I care about you, Holly."

"I know you do." Did she want more from him? This certainly wasn't the time in her life to make that kind of decision. She leaned her chin in her palms and sighed again. "Life is too complicated, Stan."

"I know." Why couldn't he find the courage to pull her close and hold her like he wanted to?

Raeleen Ost sat on her back step with her cane beside her and her hand on the dumb necklace around her neck. Bob and Price lay at her feet. Across the yard she saw the goats jumping around inside the pen. Birds sang in the trees along the driveway. Rae was watching for bluebirds. She wanted them to find the three houses Robert had set up for her. Watching birds was right up there with watching "The Price Is Right" on television. Saturday TV wasn't worth turning on except when an old movie was on.

A bird landed on the top of the nearest birdhouse. Rae frowned and squinted at it. "A sparrow!" She shook her cane and shouted, "Get off that house! That belongs to the bluebirds!" The sparrow flew away and Rae relaxed again.

She looked down at the special red button on the dumb necklace. If she pushed that button would an ambulance come racing out of town, down her road, to her driveway? She considered pushing it, then changed her mind. She didn't want to deal with anyone today, especially not someone from Life, Inc. They just might try her front door again. Besides she was wearing her oldest pair of overalls and she hadn't bothered putting on her wig. She didn't need a wig to bird watch.

With a chuckle, she looked across her yard, then she frowned. What if she fell down and had to call Life, Inc. when she wasn't wearing her wig or when she had on her ragged underwear? She moaned and Bob and Price lifted their heads and whined.

"Fiddle faddle!" Rae cried, startling a robin which had landed in the yard. "I'm not going to fall down!" But it might be a good idea to buy some new underwear and keep her wig nearby.

Just then a bird landed on the birdhouse. Rae peered closely at it and she saw the humped shoulders, the blue wings and back and the rusty-colored breast. Her heart leaped. "Bob, Price, we got us a bluebird!" Maybe she ought to press her special button just to share this great occasion with them folks at Life, Inc.

She laughed at her joke, but not loud enough to scare away the bluebird.

★   ★   ★

Carolynn looked in the mirror in Peg Graham's bathroom and laughed. Would Robert even recognize her if he saw her now? She'd done a good job of making herself look old. She didn't have to work as hard at making her self look old as she used to.

She laughed, then sobered. Robert had felt rejected because she hadn't been able to have lunch with him. Would he let her make it up to him? "Probably not," she said with a loud sigh.

With effort she pushed thoughts of Robert to the back of her mind. She had to check out Life, Inc. to see if they were legitimate. Energy and excitement surged through her. Maybe Dud was right. Maybe she couldn't quit this work.

The doorbell rang and Carolynn walked down the hall, through the living room and to the door. She grabbed the walker she'd set there and leaned on it as she opened the door.

"Lola Windess?"

"Who'd you expect? Santa Claus?"

"I'm Linus Moran. From Life, Inc." He had a medium build with cold brown eyes, brown hair, a well-trimmed mustache, and he carried a briefcase. "May I come in?"

Carolynn scowled at him. "Did you want to tell me about your product in the doorway? You think I want my snoopy neighbors to know my business?" She slowly walked away from the door, leaning heavily on the walker.

He stepped in and closed the door, then walked with her to the living room. She could smell his after-shave.

"Sit down," she said. She lowered herself to a firm armchair while he took the couch and laid his briefcase on the coffee table beside the ceramic clown.

He told her about Vital Call. She listened and asked questions. He had a pleasant voice and was kind and patient.

"I read about some woman that had Vital Call and died anyway," said Carolynn. "Marj Fletcher was her name."

"I don't remember everyone with our system, but I know there is always the chance of death being too sudden for our system to help. But it does provide help if you fall or if you have an attack and can't get to the phone to call emergency." He leaned forward and looked very earnest. "I will not sell you Vital Call if you have any qualms about it. I want you to feel comfortable and safe with our service."

"What if I take that necklace thing, then want to return it?"

"You're welcome to do that."

"It seems like a lot of money."

"I do have a special offer if you take it today." He named a sum that made her gasp. "It's a big savings, Mrs. Windess."

"What if I decide I don't want it?"

"You won't."

"Did that Marj Fletcher's husband sell back the system or did he keep it?"

"I don't recall."

"Could I buy a system that's been returned at a discount?"

Linus Moran shook his head. "What you're buying actually is our service."

"What if that red button doesn't work?"

"It does."

"What if it doesn't?"

"We haven't had that happen. We check our equipment regularly."

Carolynn sat as if she was deep in thought. "I'll take it. Where do I sign?"

"I understood your daughter wanted to help you make this decision."

Carolynn waved her hand impatiently. "She'd only complain about the cost. She wants me to move into one of those homes for seniors. Well, I won't do it! I want my own home!"

"I certainly understand that. I'm glad we can be of service. You won't be sorry you've chosen Vital Call."

"I better not be!" Carolynn struggled up, clutching the walker tightly. "Let me get my money."

"I'll hook up this device and give you this necklace. Don't press the button unless it's an emergency."

"What happens if I accidently press it?"

"Our operator will ask you what's wrong. If you're all right, you'll say so. If the operator doesn't get an answer we'll send help immediately." He glanced at his watch. "I'd better finish and get back to the office."

She watched as he hooked up the speaker box, then called Life, Inc. to tell them to start her service immediately. He turned back to her, took her money and smiled briefly.

She looked at the red button on the necklace around her neck, then pressed it.

"Don't!"

"I want to see if it works."

A woman's voice came over the speaker box and asked if Lola Windess was in trouble.

"I'm just fine," said Carolynn. "Just checking you out."

Linus Moran shook his finger at Carolynn. "Don't do that again! You know the story about the boy who cried wolf."

She nodded. "At least I know it works."

A few minutes later she opened the door to let him out, then closed it and leaned against it with a loud sigh. Suddenly the doorbell rang. She jumped, her hand at her throat. Had Moran forgotten something? She peered out the window at the side of the door. Peg's next-door neighbor, Grace O'Hare, stood there, a scowl on her round face.

Carolynn groaned. She couldn't let Grace see her this way! She raced to the bathroom, pulled off her wig, brushed her hair, washed her face, then ran back to the door. She saw the necklace still around her neck, pulled it off and quickly stuffed it in the nearest drawer, then opened the door. Grace looked ready to explode.

"Hi," said Carolynn. "I'm sorry it took so long to get here. I was in the bathroom."

"Who was the man who just left? I thought I saw an old woman in here." Grace quickly looked around. She spotted the walker and Carolynn's heart sank. "What's that?"

"A walker."

"I know that! Peg doesn't use a walker."

"I know. It's strange, isn't it?" Carolynn rubbed the shiny arm of the walker. She had to get Grace's mind off Linus Moran. "Do you think you'd ever get used to one of these if you had to use it?"

"Never!" Grace stepped back toward the door. "I just wanted to make sure everything was okay here. I told Peg I'd keep a watch on her place."

Carolynn smiled. She knew Peg had not asked Grace to water the plants because she was too nosy. "I must finish and get back home. My family is coming for dinner tomorrow."

"Tomorrow's not Easter Sunday."

"I know, but we couldn't make it for Easter, so we're doing it tomorrow."

Grace shrugged her shoulders. "I suppose when you have such a large family it is hard to get them all together at the same time."

"It sure is." Carolynn had heard that more times than she cared to admit. She held the door open wider as a hint and finally Grace left.

Carolynn ran to the bathroom, packed her case, finished the chores for Peg, then pulled out the necklace. What would happen if she pushed the red button this time? Would the operator answer? Tomorrow she'd try it again. "We'll see what happens," she said as she slipped out the door to her car.

Chapter 10

Carolynn slipped her blue-flowered apron on over the pink dress she'd worn to church, tied it, then opened the oven to check the turkey. She could tell by the smell it was almost done. She turned the fire on under the potatoes she'd peeled before they went to church. It took a lot of mashed potatoes for eighteen people.

"I'm hungry," said Robert, buttoning his red plaid shirt as he walked in. He hated leaving his suit on all day long.

"Have a slice of cake if you want." She smiled as she noticed he was looking on the counter at the two-layer chocolate cake with white icing. "I made it special for *you.*"

He smiled, but his eyes were sad.

As she lifted off the roaster lid to see if the little button in the turkey had popped up, the aroma filled the kitchen, making her mouth water. The button hadn't popped up, so she covered the turkey again and closed the oven door.

"I didn't see Flower in church this morning," said Robert as he laid a slice of the chocolate cake on his saucer.

Carolynn's stomach knotted. She'd tried several times to get Farley last night, but couldn't, then she'd tried to reach Flower, but hadn't been able to. If she'd been arrested they'd have heard it on the news. Unless Farley had kept it from the press. "I asked Holly about her, but she hasn't heard from her either. It makes me nervous, to tell you the truth."

Robert swallowed the last bite of cake and set the fork and saucer in the sink. "It's hard to sit by and do nothing to help her," he said.

Carolynn looked at him, her blue eyes wide. "I'm surprised to hear you say that. You're the one who always says to stay out of other people's business."

"Flower's practically family." He felt defensive, and her statement had angered him. "Don't *you* want to help her? You seem to be ready to help everybody else at the drop of a hat." He was thinking of Peg Graham.

Carolynn's stomach tightened once more. "Of course *I* want to help her!"

He frowned. "Meaning I never help anyone?" He wanted to remind her of Raeleen Ost, of his own children, of others who'd needed a hand, but he kept his comment to himself.

"I didn't say that!"

A muscle jumped in his jaw and he turned and stalked out of the kitchen.

Carolynn leaned weakly against the counter. She wanted to run after him and straighten the whole thing out, but she heard the front door open, then her son-in-law Kail's hearty voice and daughter Eleena's laugh. Carolynn sighed heavily. She knew Robert would speak to her only when it was necessary for the rest of the day. "So, what else is new?" she muttered as she turned the fire down under the boiling potatoes. Why hadn't she let him talk, once he started? She shouldn't have said she was surprised he wanted to do something for Flower. Would she ever learn to think before she spoke?

With a shrug, Carolynn pulled the lettuce, tomatoes, cucumbers and radishes from the refrigerator to start the salad. She knew Eleena would be in to help as soon as she spent a little time with Robert.

By the time everyone had arrived, the house seemed to rock with noise, especially when Tad, Lucy, and Jeanna gathered around the piano in the living room. Tad played and the girls sang. Before church, Carolynn and Robert had pulled out the dining room table as far as it would go and had set it with the good china. With Caro in the highchair and Heidi down for her nap that left sixteen around the table — too many to fit. Robert decided to carry in the short table and chairs he'd made for the kids several years ago. He'd put it beside the buffet and said Noah, Paige and Bobby could sit at it since they were still small enough. If Heidi woke up early she'd sit with them too. Having Stan invite Holly and her two children was nice, but it did make it more crowded.

Just before two o'clock Robert called everyone to the feast that awaited them at the table. Aromas of home cooking filled the room. The chattering stopped long enough for Robert to say the blessing. Carolynn said amen with the rest of them, then suddenly felt too tired to eat as food was passed and the chatter began again. Stan sat on her left with Holly beside him. Sixteen-year-old Tad sat at Carolynn's right with his fifteen-year-old-cousin Jeanna beside him. Tad talked with Jeanna and Stan talked with Holly, giving Carolynn a few minutes to collect her thoughts.

She glanced down the food-laden table at Robert on the other end. He was laughing at something Kate had said to him. Carolynn gripped her napkin on her lap. Robert hadn't laughed at anything she'd said in a long, long time. He didn't seem to notice that she was even in the room or at the same table. They'd have to get to the bottom of their problems! Maybe she should tell him abut working for Dumars, and about working on the Chute murder case. She shivered just thinking about telling him.

Just then Tad said something to Carolynn and she had to jerk her mind back to the family dinner.

Later in the afternoon, when Robert was taking a nap and everyone had gone except Stan, Holly, and her children, Carolynn sat on the front porch with her feet up and her head back. The porch was small, but with room enough for a glider and a few potted plants which sat along the top of the half wall. The sun was bright and warm and a gentle breeze blew. The neighborhood was quiet with only an occasional car driving past. It was not the kind of neighborhood where a murder could happen, yet it had.

Just then Holly slipped out the front door and sat down beside Carolynn.

"Hi," said Carolynn, smiling at Holly.

"I've been trying to get you alone all day!" whispered Holly. "Stan and the kids are still watching a video, so I slipped away."

"What's up?"

"Aunt Flower hired that detective."

"Lavery. I know."

Holly sighed and shook her head. "Lavery went to Indianapolis to find Mink Chute."

Carolynn twisted around in the glider to face Holly. "And?"

"Late last night Aunt Flower came over to see me. She said Lavery had called and reported that Mink and her parents were gone. The house was empty and neighbors had said they'd left just hours before."

"Did they say Mink was there?"

Holly nodded. "Yes. One of the neighbors spoke to her."

"Where is Flower today?"

"She said she knew of one other place Mink could be, but she wouldn't tell me or Lavery. She said it sounded like Mink was too terrified to stay in Indianapolis, so she took her parents and fled."

Carolynn shook her head. "I wish Flower would've confided in me."

"But she doesn't know about you."

"I know." Carolynn leaned back and glided gently back and forth beside Holly. "I wonder what frightened Mink so much that she ran?" And who was the person who'd called Farley from Hawaii? Carolynn looked unseeingly across her front yard to the quiet street.

"What will Sheriff Cobb do when he learns that Aunt Flower left town?"

Carolynn groaned. "I hope she gets back before he finds out."

"Will he arrest her?"

Carolynn was quiet a long time. "He might, Holly."

Holly moaned. "She said she couldn't sit back and do nothing. I begged her not to leave, but she wouldn't listen to me. She says if you want a job done right you have to do it yourself."

"Did she say how long she'd be gone?"

"A day, she said."

"Did she drive or fly?"

"Drove."

"So it can't be all that far." Carolynn reached for Holly's hand and squeezed it. "If the sheriff asks you about Flower you'll have to tell him."

"But I just can't!"

"Try to stay out of the sheriff's way then. If he can't find you, he can't question you."

"I'll try," Holly said in a small voice. She was quiet for several seconds. "Carolynn, you don't think Aunt Flower killed that man, do you?"

"No, I don't, Holly."

"Would you tell me if you did think so?"

"Yes. Yes, I'd tell you."

"Who did kill him? Mink? Who?"

"I'm sorry, but I don't know, Holly." Carolynn suspected both Flet and Mink, Flet more, but she didn't want to tell Holly. "Continue to pray for me and for your aunt, Holly. We want this case solved."

The front door opened and Stan stepped outside, bringing the talk between Carolynn and Holly to an abrupt end.

Stan liked seeing his mother and Holly together. "So, there you are, Holly. How about going for ice cream? Noah and Paige are all for it."

Holly forced a laugh as she jumped up. "Then I'm all for it, too. Carolynn, want to come?"

"No thanks, Holly." Carolynn glanced at Stan and saw him mouth his thanks. She hid a grin as they walked back inside.

Several minutes later Carolynn drove to Peg Graham's house and slipped quietly inside. "I hope Grace didn't see me," muttered Carolynn. She didn't feel like talking to her today.

Carolynn picked up the necklace. "Should I? Or shouldn't I?"

She touched her thumb to the red button, then pressed. The operator answered. Carolynn whispered, "I need my daughter. Call her and tell her to come right over." She'd used call forwarding to ring in at Peg's just in case the operator did call the number she'd written as Jane Withy's.

Carolynn paced the floor and waited. No call came through. She waited several more minutes then pushed the button again. Still no call came through! Vital Call was a scam! "Poor Flet! He lost Marj because of a terrible scam. What he said was true!"

She pushed the necklace back in the drawer and ran to her car. Had Flet killed Pete Chute out of anger and despair? It always came back to him. "I hate it! He's a dear, sweet man. I don't want to see him go to prison."

Back home Carolynn called Flower, but still there was no answer. Maybe Mink had killed her husband. Carolynn knew it couldn't be. Mink did not know the special place for the boning knife. Flet did. Her face pale and her fingers locked together, Carolynn turned from the phone. Should she tell Farley she suspected Flet because of what she'd learned about Vital Call?

Robert walked into the kitchen and stopped short. "What's wrong? Did something happen to one of the kids?"

Carolynn struggled to regain her composure. "No. I was just trying to reach Flower again."

"You're trembling!"

She wanted him to hold her tight. She wanted to tell him what she'd learned about Vital Call, but she couldn't without telling him everything else. "I'll be all right."

"Where were you? I looked for you and you weren't here."

"Over at Peg's."

"Her fish must eat a lot," said Robert coldly. Was there someone else in Carolynn's life? Was she meeting him at Peg's house? Jealousy ripped through Robert and he didn't know how to deal with it.

Carolynn sighed. "I have to practice my song."

A muscle tensed in Robert's jaw. He rattled the change in his pocket. "I think I'll go see how Raeleen's doing."

"Is there a problem?"

Robert shook his head. He didn't want to take time to tell Carolynn about Rae's Vital Call. If he talked too much he wouldn't be able to keep his voice from breaking. He didn't want her to know how upset she made him. "I put up bluebird houses for her. I'll see if she's spotted any bluebirds yet."

Carolynn brushed a strand of hair back. "Want me to go with you?"

Robert needed to talk to Rae alone, so he shook his head. "You have to practice."

Carolynn walked slowly to the living room, to the piano.

At Raeleen's, Robert climbed from the pickup and took a deep breath. The sun felt warm against him, but it couldn't take the chill from around his heart.

He frowned slightly as he walked toward the house. It wasn't like Rae to be indoors on such a beautiful day. He hurried his steps, suddenly frightened for her.

Just as he reached for the doorknob he heard Bob and Price barking. Rae was inside. Robert opened the door. Rae had told him a dozen times to walk right in without knocking. "Rae? It's me. you in here?"

"In here," she called in a weak voice.

He walked to the living room and found her on the couch. "Hey, what's this? You never nap."

"I wasn't this time," she snapped. "I stumbled over that rag rug and fell. I crawled here to rest a bit."

He knelt beside her and took her frail hand. She looked so small and so old! "Why didn't you call me?"

"Couldn't make it to the phone."

"Then why didn't you use this?" He touched the red button. "That's why you got it. For help."

Rae snorted. "I didn't want to use this dumb thing! You think I want them people hanging all over me?"

Robert chuckled, then sobered. "Rae, I want you to promise me you'll use this if you ever fall again. I mean it, Rae!"

Rae sighed heavily. "I don't want to swear. You know I never break my word."

"I know." He tapped the tip of her nose with his finger. "Now, swear."

She laughed weakly. "Oh, all right! I promise to use this dumb thing if I fall again. But I don't plan to fall again!"

"That's good to hear." Robert stood up, patted Bob and Price, and said, "I'm going to get you a glass of water. How about something to eat? Did you eat today?"

"I didn't. And I'm hungry as a bear! Help me to the kitchen and I'll sit at the table while you wait on me."

He lifted her easily and half-carried her to the kitchen. Once again every chair was cluttered. He cleaned one off and eased her down, then cleared another for himself. He filled a glass with cold water and handed it to her, then set the kettle on to boil for coffee.

She told him about the bluebirds as he fixed her a tuna sandwich and a cup of coffee. Bob and Price sank down on either side of her.

Robert sat beside her and sipped his coffee. Carolynn would he shocked if she knew how easily he worked in Raeleen's kitchen.

"How was the family dinner today?" asked Rae around a bite of sandwich.

"Fine. Noisy." Robert laughed. "I love my family, but it always feels good to sneak away and take a nap."

"How's Carolynn?"

Robert's face fell and he sagged back in his chair. "I don't know."

Rae could see Robert wanted to talk, so she asked the right questions, then let him talk.

Suddenly Robert jumped up and paced the kitchen. "Rae, I think she wants a divorce. I think she has someone else."

Rae shook her head. "I can't believe that. Not Carolynn. I don't know her very well, but I know how she feels about marriage and family."

"What am I going to do?" He felt five years old again, as if he were begging his mom for help.

Rae stamped her cane on the floor. "You're going to love her and cherish her and stop being fearful!" Rae rapped Robert's leg with her cane and grinned. "And it wouldn't hurt to put aside that strong, silent image and talk to her."

Robert chuckled. "I know. But it's hard to talk to her."

"So, do it anyway!"

They talked awhile longer, Robert did the chores for her, then said goodbye. "And you make sure you push that red button if you need to, Raeleen Ost!"

She wrinkled her nose and grinned.

"I want you around awhile longer. So, don't take any chances. You call for help if you need to."

"Oh, all right! You want it written in blood?"

Robert chuckled as he walked to his pickup. He hated leaving her alone as weak as she was. But she had Vital Call, so she'd be safe.

Chapter 11

Carolynn balanced a plate of turkey, dressing, mashed potatoes, corn, and carrots in one hand while she rang Flet's doorbell for the third time. Had he seen her walk up and decided not to answer? If Flet did murder Peter Chute would he also go after the others involved with Life, Inc.? She pressed the doorbell again.

"I'm coming!" Flet called from deep inside the house.

Carolynn sighed in relief as she stepped away from the screen door and waited. Robert would wonder where she was if he got back from Raeleen's before she returned home. Maybe he'd think she'd gone for a walk. She sometimes did that on Sunday afternoons.

Flet finally opened the door and stepped out on the porch. Wide white suspenders held up his navy blue pants on his skinny hips. The few strands of gray hair on top of his head stood on end. "Why do you bother with me, Carolynn?" he said as he looked down at the plate.

"No bother at all, Flet. Let's sit right here on the rockers and you eat while we visit."

He sighed heavily, then smiled slightly. "Come to think of it, I am hungry." He took the plate and they walked to the rockers and sat down.

Carolynn had changed into sneakers, jeans and a yellow sweater. She talked about the weather and the dinner with the family. Flet ate fast as if he was in a great hurry or as if he was too hungry to eat slowly.

Finally he wiped his wide mouth and long fingers with the white napkins he'd had over the top of the plate. "I have a daughter. Did you know that?"

"I sure didn't! How wonderful for you." She'd thought he only had a son — Jack. She was surprised, but pleased that he wanted to talk and didn't just send her on her way.

A boy on a bicycle rode past with a small black dog barking at the back tire. A warm breeze blew the smell of wood smoke to Carolynn from a bush at the side of the house.

Flet sighed heavily. "Some folks are determined to sow their wild oats. I was one of 'em." He folded his thin arms across his thin chest while the plate balanced on his bony knees. "Poor Marj. I don't know how she put up with me, but she did. Even when she learned about Aimee. My daughter. Aimee." He sighed again.

"I went to get Aimee that night Marj died. If I'd been home she'd have lived." His face hardened. "If that Vital Call thing would've worked, she'd still be alive."

Carolynn wasn't at all surprised to learn about Aimee. She remembered how Flet had been. "I'd think the police would investigate them."

"They won't. They wouldn't listen to me. As far as I know nobody else has complained." Flet set the plate on the porch floor and laced his long, bony fingers together. "I found out a couple of things about Life, Inc."

Carolynn's pulse jumped. She knew she couldn't appear too eager or Flet might quit talking. She said in a calm voice, "You did? What?"

Flet looked at Carolynn strangely. "You really want to know?"

She nodded. "I'm very interested."

"For one, they don't have an ambulance service like they say."

"I heard Chute once was an ambulance driver."

"Then he hired in with Life, Inc. and became a representative for Vital Call."

Carolynn wondered just how far she could go without Flet pulling away, but she decided to take a chance and be straight. "Did you go to Flower's to talk to Chute the day he was killed?"

Flet's face hardened and he barely nodded.

"Flet, did you...kill him?"

Flet turned and studied her face. "If I tell you the truth, will you believe me?"

She nodded. "Yes."

He took a deep breath and let it out slowly. "I went over after I saw Flower drive away. I knew both the Chutes were there."

"Both of them?"

He nodded. "I got the back-door key from the mat. Flower doesn't know I know about it, but I saw her take it out one day. It's the first time I used it, though. I wouldn't take advantage of knowing." Flet rubbed a large hand over his face. He looked haggard and old beyond his years.

"What happened when you walked in on the Chutes?"

Flet frowned. "She wasn't there after all and he was sitting on a kitchen chair, moaning and rubbing the back of his head like he'd been hit. I wanted to strangle him where he sat!"

"But you didn't."

"No. He jumped up when he saw me. He didn't even remember who I was." Flet knotted his fists, then slowly relaxed them and pressed his hands to his thin legs. "So, I told him. And I told him Marj was dead because of him and his bogus Vital Call."

Carolynn could barely sit still, but she forced herself to stay calm. "Then what?"

"He pulled a pack of M & Ms from his pocket and started eating them as if it didn't matter that Marj was dead. I slapped them out of his hand and they scattered across the floor. Then he got mad and he made me pick 'em up. I was bigger than him, but he was stronger and a whole lot younger." He groaned as he remembered the humiliation. "So, I picked 'em up. He pointed to a few by the sink counter that I'd missed. He pushed me down and told me to get them all." Flet's cheeks paled even more. "I was mad enough to kill him! When I was down there I remembered about Flower's boning knife."

Carolynn held her breath. Her nerve ends jangled. The rocker creaked as Flet moved.

"I opened the door and pulled out the knife. Chute was sure surprised. He yelled at me to drop it. But I didn't. I wanted to ram it right through him, but before I could, somebody grabbed me from behind. A big man, taller than me, but I couldn't see him, only feel that he was taller and broader. He twisted the knife from my hand and it fell to the floor. He strangled me and I blacked out." Flet rubbed his throat as if he could feel the pain again. "When I came to, Chute was dead on the floor and I was the only one in the house. I picked up the rest of the M & Ms and I got out of there fast."

Carolynn moistened her suddenly dry lips. "How'd the other man get in?"

"I'd left the back door ajar." Flet shot a look at Carolynn. "You won't tell the sheriff, will you? He'll assume I killed Chute. But I didn't, Carolynn. Honest to God, I didn't. I think that man did. Or Mink could've been hiding in another room and she did it. But I didn't!"

Carolynn patted his hand to let him know she believed him. Oh, but he'd opened a can of worms! He'd left the knife out in plain sight for anyone to use.

"I felt like killing him, but I thought of Aimee and Jack and I knew I had them to live for. Jack still doesn't know about Aimee. But we're all three going to have dinner together at the Olive Garden Tuesday night and hopefully we can be a family, not just three people apart from each other. Do you think it can work?"

"Anything's possible if you want it badly enough."

"And I want my family." His voice broke.

They sat in silence for a while, then Carolynn asked, "Do you have any idea who the man was that knocked you out?"

"I have an idea."

Carolynn's muscles tensed. "Who?"

Flet shook his head. "I want to take care of this myself."

"How?"

"Getting evidence against him to give to the sheriff."

"I could help you."

"You, Carolynn?"

She flushed. Sometimes it was very hard to stay undercover! "I want to help, Flet. Who would suspect me if I went around asking questions?"

"It's awful dangerous, Carolynn."

She shrugged. "Not if I don't get caught."

Flet rubbed his face again. "I been trying to get in the office at Life, Inc. to go over their records. I did learn that Linus Moran and Weldon Tremayne have only had this business here in town about three weeks. I want to know where they were before they came here."

"I can find that out."

"Then you find out for me, will you? I figure if I can get this settled, then I can let Marj go. I can get on with life with Aimee and Jack."

"I'll do what I can." Carolynn stood up to go. She picked up the place and smiled. "Be careful, Flet."

"You too. And thanks for the dinner. It was mighty tasty. But don't bother doing it again. I can manage on my own."

"I'll bring something again tomorrow." She laughed and he joined in.

She walked slowly away from his house, the plate in her hand. Had Flet told her the truth? Of course he had! Had the man killed Chute? Or had Mink?

Monday morning Carolynn took the necklace with the red button and the speaker and walked into the plush office of Life, Inc. Floy Tedmund looked up with a smile. She wore a pale yellow wool suit with an olive-green blouse. A bouquet of spring flowers sat on the desk near her phone. The smile died as she saw the necklace and speaker.

"Jane Withy, isn't it?" asked Floy in her perfect voice.

Carolynn nodded. "I brought this back!" She held up the necklace. "I want to see Linus Moran now!"

Floy pressed her hands on her desk and her inch-long nails shot out their bright flames of red. "But he's not here. Could I help you?"

"Do you own this company?"

"Well, no."

"Then you can't help me." Carolynn started around the desk to the offices beyond, but Floy immediately blocked her way. Carolynn scowled at her and said in her sternest voice, "You tell Mr. Moran to get out here right now!"

"He is not here, Mrs. Withy. But Weldon Tremayne is."

"Does he own the company?"

"Yes. Along with Linus."

"Then I'll talk to him."

"Please, have a seat and I'll speak with him."

Acting very reluctant and very angry, Carolynn sat on the nearest chair. It was comfortable, but she didn't sink back and relax.

Floy picked up the phone and spoke into it. Finally she put it down and said, "He'll be right out."

A tall man who looked as if he lifted weights walked from the back and up to Carolynn. He was probably in his forties and he had dark, neatly cut hair, a pleasant smile and he dressed very well. "May I help you, Mrs. Withy? May I call you Jane?"

She jumped up. "You can call me anything you want as long as you give back my mother's money. She doesn't need this nor does she want it!" Carolynn shook the necklace.

"But she signed an agreement."

"Rip it up!"

"It's not that easy."

"It had better be that easy! She doesn't have money to burn, you know!"

"We gave her a very good deal."

"Either I get her money back or I go to the newspaper and tell them you took advantage of an old lady's fear."

Weldon Tremayne looked startled, but quickly masked it.

Floy cleared her throat.

Tremayne shot her a look, then turned back to Carolynn. "Why don't we go to my office and talk?"

Floy Tedmund scowled at Carolynn as she followed Tremayne around the desk and to the back. There were three doors, one probably to a bathroom, that Carolynn wanted to peek behind, but she followed Tremayne.

Tremayne's office was almost bare, not at all plush like the reception area. A lap-top computer sat in the middle of the desk and a telephone beside it. Tremayne motioned Carolynn to a straight-back chair while he sat behind his desk. "Now, what seems to be the trouble?"

"Just how long have you had this business?"

"Two years. Since Vital Call was first developed."

"But not two years here in Middle Lake."

"No."

"How long here?"

"Fairly new."

"How long?"

"Three weeks. But we're all settled in and plan to be here a good long while."

"Where were you before that?"

"Pine Ridge."

"That's near Lansing?"

"Yes."

"Well, the thing costs too much and I want my mother's money back."

Tremayne narrowed his dark eyes. "She gets very good service for the cost."

"Not enough for the price you charged! Mom said she gave you cash. Cash is what I want back."

"Can I say anything to change your mind?"

"No! I want the agreement torn up and the cash returned."

Tremayne's eyes flashed as he jerked open his drawer. "You're fortunate that we haven't made it to the bank this morning." He held out the money and she took it.

"The agreement also," said Carolynn.

"I'm doing this only because we refuse to have a customer who isn't satisfied." He opened a side drawer of his desk and pulled out the agreement. He tore it in half, then handed it to Carolynn.

"I'm sure mine is not your first complaint," she said as she pushed the agreement and the money into her large purse.

"Our customers are very satisfied." Tremayne walked to the door. "I'm very busy, Mrs. Withy."

"Yes. I'm sure you are." She walked into the hall, then glanced at the desk where Floy sat. Christine Lavery was talking to Floy! Carolynn struggled to keep her composure. Lavery! She had long black hair, blue eyes that didn't miss a thing, and was good at her job. Lavery had tried the past five yeas she'd worked for Dumars Investigative Services to prove that Carolynn was more than a secretary. If Lavery saw her now she wouldn't hesitate to make trouble for her.

"Now what's wrong?" asked Tremayne impatiently.

"Do you have a back entrance?" asked Carolynn in a low voice. "I don't want anybody knowing my mother did business with you."

Tremayne sighed. "Down the hall and to your left."

Carolynn walked quickly past the offices and slipped around the corner. She opened the door, then closed it without going out. Her pulse quickened. Slowly she walked back and peered around the corner. The hall was empty. Tremayne and Floy were both talking to Lavery near the door of the outer office.

Carolynn inched her way to the nearest office, carefully opened the door and slipped inside. With a frown, she looked around. The room was totally empty. Maybe this had been Peter Chute's office. They had certainly cleared it out fast.

Carolynn opened the door enough to see that the hall was still empty. If Tremayne or Floy turned they'd see her. She'd tell them she was looking for a bathroom. But would they believe her? If Lavery saw her it would be the end of everything. Carolynn eased out and down to the door across from Tremayne. She opened it to find it was also empty. She frowned. She crept back to the exit and slipped outside, her heart lodged in her throat. Why were the offices empty? Was Life, Inc. getting ready to leave Middle Lake?

Carolynn walked through the alley behind the row of businesses, then around to the street where her car was parked. Just as she reached her car Lavery walked out of the building.

"Snooping again, Carolynn Burgess?" called Lavery.

Carolynn turned and forced a smile. "Lavery! What brings you to this part of town?"

"Business. And you?"

Carolynn shrugged. "Any word from Dud and Meg?"

"They're on holiday."

"I know."

Lavery flipped back her long hair. "Are you here to see the people at Life, Inc.?"

Carolynn's stomach cramped. "What makes you think that?"

"I know Flower Graidal is a friend of yours and I know how you like to put your nose in where it doesn't belong." Lavery narrowed her eyes and took a step toward Carolynn. "Well, just back off! This is my case and I don't need you snooping it it."

"How is Flower?"

Lavery snapped, "I suppose you asked that because you know she left Saturday and isn't back yet."

"Oh?"

"Don't look so innocent! I know Holly Loudan told you." Lavery smiled. "Just how are Holly and Stan doing?"

Carolynn shrugged. "Fine."

"They are seeing each other, aren't they?"

"That isn't your business." Stan had taken Lavery out a few times before she'd gotten married. Carolynn had objected, but had managed to keep it to herself. Lavery somehow sensed it, though.

"Tell Stan hello for me. He's a nice guy, but it's too bad he's such a mama's boy."

Carolynn's temper shot up. She bit back the ugly words that were on the tip of her tongue.

Lavery laughed mockingly. "I must be running." She slipped into her white Toyota and drove away.

"Good riddance," Carolynn muttered under her breath as she unlocked her car.

Chapter 12

Monday afternoon Carolynn quickly dried her hands after finishing lunch dishes and answered the phone on the third ring.

"She's back," said Holly in a low voice.

"Flower?"

"Yes. Just got in. And she brought Mink and her parents with her."

"Where are they now?"

"At my place. I must go. My boss is frowning at me."

Carolynn heard the click of Holly hanging up, then she set the receiver in place, her mind racing. She'd get right over to Holly's and speak with Flower and Mink. How had Flower convinced Mink to return with her? And what story would Mink tell?

Carolynn tugged her unbuttoned, blue plaid flannel shirt down over her jeans, then straightened the collar of her white blouse. Maybe she'd have the case solved by tonight. She smiled and started toward the closet.

Just then Robert walked up from the basement and stopped her in the hallway. He wore his new jeans and a gray sweat shirt. "Carolynn, we need to talk," he said in a no-nonsense voice. He walked her to the kitchen, his hand at her back. "I wanted to at lunch, but with Stan here, I couldn't."

Carolynn glanced at the clock on the microwave. She had to see Flower and Mink before Lavery got there to complicate things. "Robert, could we please make it later?"

"No!" He rubbed an unsteady hand over his jaw. "We've put if off long enough."

Because of Lavery, Carolynn knew she'd have to refuse Robert even though she didn't want to. She could see he was upset, but speaking with Flower and Mink was crucial to the case. "A couple more hours won't hurt. Flower's back and I must go see her."

"Flower can wait!"

Panic rose in Carolynn. She had to beat Lavery to see Flower, but she couldn't tell Robert that. Carolynn caught Robert's hand and held it to her heart. "Please, can we make this later? I must see Flower now."

Robert jerked away. "What is this terrible secret you're keeping from me?"

"It's no big deal."

"Are you seeing another man?"

Carolynn burst out laughing. "What? How ridiculous!"

The color drained from Robert's face. "Don't laugh at me."

"I'm sorry."

"I'm hurting. Can't you see that?"

Carolynn stared at him in surprise. "You're serious!"

He nodded as he quickly brushed moisture from his eyes. He'd been thinking about what to say to Carolynn since he'd spoken to Rae. Finally he'd found the courage and he didn't want to waste another second. "It's eating me alive."

"Robert, you're the only man for me! I can't believe you'd even suggest differently."

"What else should I think with you acting the way you have been?"

She glanced at the clock, then at Robert. She couldn't walk out on him even to speak with Flower and Mink. Carolynn reached out for Robert, but he turned away and sank to a kitchen chair. Silently she prayed for the right words.

"I know I haven't been the best husband in the world," he said hoarsely.

"Robert! I love you!" She sat beside him where Stan always sat. "I do! But you must know it."

"Then why were you going to ask me for a divorce?"

She gasped, her hand over her heart. "I wasn't! Whatever gave you that ridiculous idea?"

"The other day you said you had something to say to me that would upset me. What was that?"

She flushed painfully. "It had nothing to do with divorce."

"Then what was it?"

"There's no reason to tell you now. Things have changed."

"Things?"

She slipped an arm around his back and rested her head on his arm. She smelled sawdust and sweat. "Robert, I would never want out of our marriage. We've had our ups and downs, but we both agreed when we got married that it was for life. I would never go back on that vow."

"I know you're not happy."

"Only because I want that spark back. I want to feel your love, not just take it for granted. I want us to talk. I mean, really talk." She lifted her head. "I want the passion back."

Robert looked into her eyes. Dare he believe her? "I can still see a secret lurking in there."

She bit her lower lip. "It's my work, Robert. Secrets from my work. You know I can't tell you what goes on there." She felt a flush starting up her neck and she tried to force it down, but it crawled up her neck and over her face and burned her ears.

Robert jumped up, his eyes dark with pain. "You're in love with Dud, aren't you?"

"What? No!"

"And you've been meeting with him at Peg's house."

"Robert! What a terrible, terrible thing to think! I'm a Christian! I would never do that!"

His face ashen, Robert reached for the phone. "I'll call him right now and have it out with him."

"You can't," said Carolynn weakly.

"I will!" Robert scooped up the phone.

"He and Meg are on vacation. For a month."

"Is that the truth?"

"Yes! Robert, what has gotten into you? I can't believe you'd suspect me of being unfaithful to you! It's so ridiculous, it's laughable."

"I'm not laughing." He dropped the receiver in place with a loud clatter.

Carolynn rubbed her hands across her cheeks, then clasped them at her throat. "You'd better look at this correctly, Robert Burgess! Satan is a liar and a deceiver. He put these lies in your mind to upset you and to tear you up. Don't believe him!"

"But you said you had a secret to tell me."

Carolynn pressed her hands to her burning cheeks. She'd have to tell him the truth. She couldn't let him continue to suffer even if she had to endure his anger by telling him the truth. She sighed heavily. "You might as well sit down for this, Robert."

Fear gripped him and he wanted to run from the kitchen, but he sat down and steeled himself for what she had to say.

She tugged at the neckline of her blouse to give her more air. "Robert, it's about my job."

He frowned. Why was she bringing up her job at such a time as this?

She locked her icy fingers together in front of her on the table and stared down at a chipped spot on the clear nail polish on her right thumb. "I have not been the secretary at Dumars Investigative Services."

"What does that have to do with anything."

"Everything! Let me finish." Her throat felt bone-dry.

"What have you been doing at Dumars all these years then?"

She took a long, deep, steadying breath and let it out slowly. "I've been an undercover investigator."

Speechlessly, he stared at her. Who was this stranger in Carolynn's body?

She clasped and unclasped her hands. "I didn't tell you because I knew you wouldn't like it. I was afraid you'd force me to quit. And I love the work, Robert!"

"Are you still doing it?" he said weakly.

She nodded. "I'm trying to find Peter Chute's killer."

"I thought Flower hired Lavery."

"She did. I'm doing this as a favor for a special friend."

"Who?"

Carolynn hesitated. "Holly."

"Holly Loudan?"

"She learned my secret when she was in high school. But thankfully she kept the secret."

Robert groaned. "So I wasn't the only one in the dark?"

Carolynn shook her head. She felt weighted down with Robert's anguish. "Dud knows, of course. Holly. And the sheriff."

"The sheriff of Middle Lake knows you?"

"Yes."

Robert wiped a trembling hand over his face. "This is too much to take in."

"I know it's a shock. I decided that I'd quit working for Dud, and not have to tell you any of this, but Holly came over after she found Chute with Flower's boning knife sticking in his chest and I couldn't turn her down."

"Do you know how to solve a murder?"

"Yes."

Robert threw up his hands, then let them fall limply to his sides.

"I'm sorry to upset you so much."

"Upset! I don't even know what to say!"

"I'm sorry," she whispered.

He scowled at her. "Did you ever come close to getting killed?"

She didn't want to tell him, but she nodded, then quickly added, "But I never did!" She laughed at the sound of that. "I never got hurt too badly."

"I can't believe this, Carolynn! I just can't!

"I know. I'm sorry. I don't know what else to say."

"*You* don't? I've lost the few words I had!"

She glanced at the clock. It was almost two! "I don't want to leave you now, Robert, but will you be all right if I do?"

He shrugged. He had a lot to sort through. Right now his brain was whirling out of control.

"We'll talk again when I get home." Carolynn looked helplessly at him, then ran to get her jacket and purse.

Outdoors, a cool wind tugged at her dark blonde curls. A robin flew up from the lawn and landed on a budding lilac.

A few minutes later Carolynn reached Holly's house, but frowned when she saw Lavery's car already there. With a sigh, she pulled up beside Lavery's car and behind Flower's '76 Corvette, then slowly walked to the side door. She'd have to be very careful of what she said. Even though Robert knew the truth about her she didn't want others to know, especially Lavery.

Carolynn steeled herself, breathed a prayer for help and knocked.

Flower opened the door almost immediately. She wore a flowing fuchsia jacket over black slacks and a bright yellow blouse. Her long earrings were yellow and fuchsia. "Carolynn! What brings you here? Holly's at work."

"I know. She called to say you were here. She knew how worried I've been."

"Come in. Lavery's here talking to Mink Chute and her parents."

"We won't bother her then," said Carolynn. She'd wanted a chance to speak to Flower privately.

"Come in the kitchen for coffee. I just made a fresh pot. Lavery's in the front room with the others, so we won't disturb them at all."

"Good."

A few minutes later Carolynn sat across the table from Flower with a cup of coffee in her hand. "How did you ever convince Mink and her parents to return with you?"

"It took a lot of talking." Flower shook her head, sending her earrings dancing on her slender shoulders.

"Her parents didn't want to come here, nor have her return. I told Mink that the sheriff suspected me of killing Pete."

"Did Mink know he was dead?"

"Yes."

"How did she learn of it?"

"On the news, she said."

"But she ran before it was on the news."

"She intended to leave him and stay with her parents."

"So why did they all run?"

Flower frowned slightly. "They didn't exactly run, Carolynn. They went to Mink's special hideaway up north just to stay away from the press."

"I see."

"Mink is very upset about Pete's death."

Carolynn urged Flower to talk about Mink and her parents, then at a lull in the conversation, she said, "I learned that Flet saw Chute and Mink at your place."

"He did? But I thought he was away."

"He didn't go to his son's after the funeral."

"Did he tell the sheriff?"

"Yes." Carolynn knew he hadn't told about going inside Flower's house, though, and taking out the boning knife. "Flower, when you returned the day of the murder to pick up Mink after her talk with her husband, did she seem frightened or hurt or agitated in any way?"

Flower nodded. "She seemed frightened, of course. She told me yesterday that she'd been in a great deal of pain from Pete hitting her in the stomach, but she didn't want to alarm me so she didn't say anything at the time."

"Did she hit Pete back?" Carolynn was thinking about what Flet had said about Chute rubbing his head in pain.

Flower frowned. "Why are you asking me all these questions?"

"Because she's a snoop," snapped Lavery from the doorway. She wore a charcoal-gray suit with a pale-green, silk blouse and high-heeled black shoes. "What're you doing here, Carolynn? Aside from snooping?"

Carolynn managed to smile. "I came to see Flower."

"Don't give her any information," said Lavery, tossing her mane of black hair over her slender shoulder.

"Don't worry. She didn't," said Carolynn, her sneakers quiet on the tile floor as she carried her empty cup to the sink. She rinsed it out and put it in the dishwasher.

Just then Mink and her parents walked in. Flower introduced them to Carolynn. Mink was quite attractive, about thirty years old, and wore jeans and a light-weight red sweater over a red plaid blouse. Max Goodbody was of medium build, nice looking with a haunted look in his brown eyes. His wife, Jill, looked like an older version of Mink only with short hair and pale skin. In her mind's eye Carolynn matched the strand of long hair that she'd found in Flower's spare bedroom to Mink's. They matched. Once Farley saw Mink and heard her story he'd believe Flower.

Carolynn passed the time of day with Mink and her parents while Lavery walked restlessly around the kitchen with a cup of steaming coffee in her hand, her heels clicking loudly on the tile.

Finally Lavery set her empty cup on the counter and said, "Flower, I'd like to speak with you for a while. Mr. and Mrs. Goodbody and Mink, I'd like to have you with us."

Carolynn toyed with her black leather purse, but didn't make a move to leave even though she knew Lavery wanted her to.

With a frown, Lavery walked away with the others following. Carolynn caught Mink's arm and stopped her. Mink lifted her brow questioningly.

"I'd like to speak with you," whispered Carolynn. "Tell Lavery you're going to the bathroom."

Mink hesitated, then asked Lavery to excuse her for a while. She turned to Carolynn. "Flower has spoken a great deal about you and your friendship."

"We're good friends."

"What did you want of me?"

"I just wanted to say I'm sorry about your husband," whispered Carolynn.

"I didn't want him to die," she murmured.

"I'm sure you didn't." Carolynn led Mink away from the connecting doors. She looked Mink right in the eye. "He hit you that day, didn't he? And you hit him back."

Mink's eyes filled with tears as she nodded. "I grabbed that piece of petrified rock that Flower uses as a book end for her cookbooks and I hit him with that. I was so afraid he was dead that I left him right there on the floor. I drove his car in the garage and let Flower think he was already gone."

"Did you see Fletcher Raabe that day?"

"Who?"

"He lives near Flower. Your husband sold his wife Vital Call and it didn't work, and she died."

Mink dabbed at her eyes. "Oh, yes, I remember now! When I learned it was all a scam, I told Pete to get out of that business." She looked as if she would burst into tears at any moment. "But he wouldn't."

"So you didn't see Flet Raabe while you were at Flower's?"

"No. Why do you ask?"

Carolynn shrugged. "Your parents seem very concerned about you."

"They are. They're glad I'm finally free of Pete."

"But sorry it took murder to do it?"

"Yes. I sometimes was afraid daddy would kill Pete with his bare hands."

"But they were both in Indianapolis when Pete died."

"Of course. Where else would they be?"

"Did you think you were in danger from the folks at Vital Call?"

Mink nodded.

"Daddy had me call the sheriff and say I was in Hawaii on vacation so I wouldn't be accused of killing Pete or blamed for the truth coming out about Vital Call."

"And was the truth coming out?"

"I heard Floy and the men talking about it the day before I left Pete."

"Did you tell Lavery all of this?"

"Yes."

"Did she set up a meeting with the sheriff?"

With a shiver, Mink nodded. "We're going in to see him in just a few minutes."

"Do you know who killed your husband?"

"No. Unless it was one of his partners from Vital Call. They knew he was coming to talk to me and they knew I wanted him out of the business. Maybe they thought he'd give in and leave."

"Maybe." Carolynn hadn't considered that motive.

"I'd better get back in with Lavery."

"Don't mention you spoke to me. Lavery doesn't like me at all and so she doesn't want me to know what's going on with any of her cases."

"Flower is impressed with her."

"So I noticed." Carolynn smiled. "Thanks for talking with me. I have a good shoulder to cry on if ever you need to talk."

"Thanks. I'll remember that."

Carolynn watched her walk away, then let herself out and drove slowly back home. Would Farley believe Mink's story? Or would he arrest her?

Carolynn shook her head. She liked Mink and didn't believe she'd killed her husband. But she could've left the car in the garage, slipped back inside in time to see Flet with the boning knife. Maybe she jumped up on a chair to hit him, grabbed the knife and stabbed Pete. "That doesn't work at all," muttered Carolynn.

She parked in her garage, then sank low in her seat as she remembered what was facing her inside. "Oh, Robert, what will you do now?"

Chapter 13

Carolynn slowly walked into the house, then stopped at the closed basement door and listened for Robert. No sounds of sawing or sanding or pounding came up. "Robert?" she called. She called twice more, then looked out to see if his pickup was still there. He had a special place to park it since she and Stan used the garage. The pickup was gone and she sighed. Had he gone off somewhere to think or to deliver more birdhouses? Maybe Raeleen Ost had called to tell him about more bluebirds at her place.

"I hope he's over his anger when he gets back," Carolynn muttered as she walked to the kitchen. She spotted a note on the refrigerator in Robert's sprawl: *"Rae needs help with chores. R."*

"Good. It'll give me time to go to Dumars."

Carolynn pulled a jug of orange juice from the refrigerator, unscrewed the lid, looked at it and shrugged, then drank about four swallows right from the jug. She set it back in place, dabbed her mouth with the corner of the dish towel just as Stan walked in. She jumped guiltily. She'd said more times than she could remember, "Never drink out of the jug! Others don't want your germs or your backwash." Hopefully Stan hadn't seen her.

Stan stabbed his fingers through his hair, spiking it, then flattened it down. He had dark circles under his eyes. He wore jeans and a tee-shirt that said "JESUS IS THE REAL ROCK." "I'm glad you're here, mom."

"I was just going out."

He slipped his arms around her and hugged her close. "Mom, I think I'm in love."

She chuckled. "As if that's news to me."

He stepped away from her and once again stabbed his fingers through his hair. "With Holly."

"No kidding."

"Mom!"

"Have you told her?"

"I can't! I won't until I know."

Carolynn reached up and kissed Stan's cheek. He needed a shave. "I'm sure you've been praying about this."

"Yes. But I still don't have an answer!"

"Do you really want an answer?"

He frowned at her. "You know I do."

"Don't let fear stop you from hearing the answer, Stanley Burgess!"

He sighed heavily. "I guess that is what's happening. Sometimes I think she really cares. And other times I just don't know."

"She's under a lot of pressure right now with the murder."

"I know. And Paul Caine won't leave her alone." Stan jabbed his right fist into his left palm. "I'd like to —" He sagged to a kitchen chair. "Who am I trying to fool? I'm all talk and no action. The only action in my life is what I put in my books!"

Carolynn sat beside him and slipped her arm around him. "Stan, you can be a man of action."

"Sure. You bet."

Carolynn tapped his arm. "You must make the first step."

"That's the hard part."

"You know in your heart you love Holly. Tell her! What can she do? Shoot you?"

Robert turned a haggard face to Carolynn. "She can tell me to get lost!"

"And will that kill you?"

"It'll feel like it."

"It might make you feel bad, but you'll still be alive and you'll go on living. But if you don't speak to her, you'll continue in your misery, wondering what she'd say or do if you did talk to her. Not knowing can eat you alive."

"You're right about that."

"Stan, you came to talk to me about this because you knew what I'd say. You knew I'd tell you to talk to Holly. So, you must want to talk to her. You just needed a nudge."

Stan rubbed his hand across his jaw. "Why is it I'm having such a hard time with this? Wes, Leena, and Christa fell in love and got married while they were in their early twenties. "I don't have a wife or a family. I don't even have a house of my own!"

"Stan, you can have all of that if you want. But you can't have any of those things if you bury yourself right here in this house, up in your rooms." Carolynn smoothed back his thick brown hair. "You aren't going to fail if you try, Stan. And if you do, so what? We all fail from time to time, but we keep on trying. If you don't try, you can't accomplish anything. Your stories would never sell if you stuck them in your desk drawer and left them there."

"I know. But a story is different. It's only a story. We're talking about my life!"

Carolynn caught Stan's hand and held it between hers. His hand was so much like Robert's! She'd never noticed that before. He was so much like Robert! "Stan, never forget that God is with you. He'll help you find the right wife. He'll help you get a home. He cares about every area of your life."

"I know, mom." Stan sighed heavily. "I guess this is one part of my life I've not turned over to Him."

"You must!"

He nodded.

"Stan, it's right for you to marry and have a home of your own. You'll make a wonderful husband and father!"

"But what if I don't? I'm not like Wes."

"I'll admit your brother is very outgoing. But you can't compare the two of you. You're Stan. He's Wes. Both of you have talents and strengths. Both of you have weaknesses. But you can never compare yourself with him. Measure yourself only with yourself. Be the best Stanley Burgess you can be. And as Stanley you're never alone, you have God to help you succeed."

"I love you, mom."

"I love you." She kissed his cheek, then dabbed tears from her eyes. When she was young she'd thought her job of mothering would be over when her children turned eighteen. How wrong she'd been! She'd be a mother to them and would mother them all of her life. And she was glad even if at times she felt overwhelmed with the responsibility. "Now, I want you to go see Holly tonight and tell her just how you feel!"

"I think I will!" Stan grinned. "Even if I shiver in my boots. I'll do it anyway."

"And if Paul Caine tries to get in your way, toss him out on his ear." Carolynn chuckled and Stan laughed and hugged her hard.

Several minutes later, after Stan ran back upstairs to work, Carolynn called Jay Sommers at Dumars to set up a meeting with him. But first she had to get through Mable Greene.

"Mable, I have a message from Dud he asked me to give to Jay."

"Jay's on another line right now," said Mable crisply.

"Then I'll wait."

"Give me the message and I'll relay it to Jay."

Carolynn gripped the receiver tighter. "Mable, I must speak with Jay. In fact, I want an appointment with him. In ten minutes."

"That's impossible!"

"I know better." Carolynn forced back her frustration. "Look, Mable. I have worked with you. You know I wouldn't set up a meeting with Jay unless it was necessary."

"You mean you want to hire him?"

"No, Mable. I want to talk with him. In ten minutes. I'll be right there." She hung up before Mable could argue further. "How can Dud put up with her?" But Carolynn knew Mable was excellent at her job or Dud wouldn't keep her on.

Ten minutes later, Carolynn walked through the heavy glass door into Dumar's Investigative Services. She still wore her sneakers and her jeans, but had slipped a green pullover sweater on and left her flannel shirt at home. She looked toward the desk in the small reception area. Mable stood at the file behind the desk. Several ivy plants hung on a plant tree. "I'm here, Mable," Carolynn sang out.

"Jay will be right with you," said Mable stiffly. She was in her late twenties, tall, big-boned with thick blonde hair cut short. She wore a calf-length, multicolored skirt with a wide black belt around her thick waist and a silky black blouse. She didn't believe in wearing jewelry, not even a watch. And she didn't believe in wasting time or energy. "Have a chair." She pointed to the four cushioned chairs lining the wall.

"Thank you," said Carolynn, but she didn't move.

Just then a light blinked on Mable's phone and she picked it up and said, "Yes." She listened, then hung up. "Go right in."

Carolynn walked toward Jay's office. It was between Dud's and Lavery's. When Carolynn reached his door she glanced over her shoulder to see Lavery walking to the glass door. Carolynn's heart sank. Lavery would've seen her car in the parking lot. She quickly stepped inside Jay's small office and locked the door.

"Hello, Carolynn." Jay leaned on his desk and looked from her to the locked door with a twinkle in his hazel eyes. He was short and slight with brick-red hair and freckles on freckles. He was the youngest and newest detective at Dumars and usually dressed in loose-fitting jeans and polo shirts.

Carolynn laughed breathlessly as she walked toward him. She noticed the red stripe on his polo shirt clashed with his red hair. She knew a thing like that wouldn't bother him. "I need a few minutes of your time without Lavery interrupting."

"You got it." Jay waved her to an oak chair and she sat down. "So, what has Lavery been up to this time? Reading your mail? Bugging your phone?"

"She thinks I've been snooping in her case."

"And have you?"

Carolynn grinned and shrugged. "Maybe I better show you this before we talk further." She pulled Dud's letter from her purse and handed it to Jay.

He cocked a red brow as he looked at Carolynn. Finally he took the note and read it. He chuckled. "So, Lavery has been right all along."

Carolynn nodded. "I still want my real work here kept confidential."

"That's great! You got my word on it."

Carolynn knew he was a man of his word and she relaxed a little.

"I think you can accomplish more that way. I can use you on a case I'm working on."

"Right now I need your help with a case I'm working on. The Peter Chute murder."

Jay slapped his leg and laughed hard. "You really do have it in for Lavery, don't you?"

"Not at all!" His words stung Carolynn because she knew it was too close to the truth. Impatiently, she pushed those thoughts aside. This was not the time to deal with her feelings and actions toward Lavery.

"Why don't you two work together on this?"

"She'd never keep my work a secret."

"You're right about that. She'd hire a plane to write it in the sky."

"She would."

"Let her solve it alone."

Carolynn lifted her chin and her eyes flashed. "I can't!"

"A contest, eh?"

"I just want to solve this case, Jay. Are you familiar with it at all?"

"Lavery has talked to me about it."

"I believe someone from Life, Inc. killed Chute. I need you to get into their office and check their files. And run a check on the three people involved with the company." She handed him a list of their names. "I don't believe they have an ambulance service nor do they make the calls they promise to make." She told him about her disguise as Lola Windess and what she'd seen when she'd returned the system as Jane Withy. "I don't know what kind of security system they use at their office, but I know you can handle anything."

He grinned and raised his red brows. "I do my best."

"I need a list of all the people who've bought Vital Call. Someone will have to let them know the truth.

And do it before someone else dies." Carolynn told him about Marj Raabe. "Can you take care of this today?"

Jay nodded. "But only if you help me with this case I'm working on. Nursing home fraud. You're perfect for it and it won't take much time. But it is risky. Fair trade, Carolynn."

Carolynn wondered if Robert would ever speak to her again if she took the job Jay suggested. She'd have to take that chance. Reluctantly she agreed.

Just then Lavery called to Jay and rattled his doorknob. "Let me in, Jay."

Carolynn frowned.

"I can't," called Jay. "Carolynn Burgess is in here trying to convince me to let her work as a detective instead of a secretary."

Carolynn bit back a gasp.

Jay winked at her and grinned.

Lavery hit the door, then all was quiet.

"I guess she left," said Jay with a wicked chuckle. "What else can I do for you?"

"I also need you to call the travel bureau about Max Goodbody, Mink Chute's dad, and get them to tell you the flight he and the family took from Indianapolis. Probably Saturday."

Jay punched the number, talked for a while, listened, then said, "Maybe it was another day then. Check it for me, will you?" He listened, then slowly hung up. "Max Goodbody flew to Grand Rapids last Thursday morning early, but never used his return ticket."

Carolynn leaned forward, her hands over her purse on her lap. "Thursday? The day of the murder? He was supposedly at home until Saturday when he, his wife and Mink flew up north." Carolynn narrowed her eyes. "I wonder. He had motive and now we learn he could've had opportunity. I think I'd better talk to him."

"Do you want me to share this bit of news with Lavery?"

Carolynn flushed. "No. Let her find it out herself."

Jay laughed and Carolynn walked out with her cheeks red.

Lavery stopped her at the heavy glass door. Sparks shot from Lavery's blue eyes. "You'd better not be messing with my case, Burgess! I'm close to solving it and I don't want you to get in the way."

"I won't get in your way," said Carolynn coldly.

"I didn't appreciate you questioning Flower and Mink awhile ago at Holly's."

"I talked to them."

"Questioned them!" snapped Lavery. Then she flipped back her mass of black hair. "You might as well know the sheriff said he is going to arrest the killer soon."

Carolynn's stomach knotted. "So, who does he plan to arrest?"

"Not Flower." Lavery smiled smugly. "It's someone you wouldn't know about. Someone at Life, Inc."

"Just how did that *someone* find the boning knife?"

Lavery angrily pushed open the door. "How should I know?"

Carolynn bit back further words and walked to her car.

Later Carolynn parked beside Flower's Corvette and walked to Holly's back door. Paige and Noah were already home from school and Holly would soon be home from work.

Paige answered the door, then flew into Carolynn's arms. "Did you know Aunt Flower's back? But she forgot to bring me anything. She said next time."

Carolynn laughed as she walked to the kitchen with Paige chattering beside her. Flower, Mink and the

Goodbodys were in the kitchen drinking coffee. Noah sat in the corner reading a book.

"Why, Carolynn! Twice in one day," said Flower, smiling as she jumped up. "Would you like a cup of coffee?"

"No, thanks. But I would like to speak privately with you, Mr. Goodbody."

"Why?" asked Mink in alarm.

Carolynn smiled. "It's nothing to be upset about."

"Carolynn's a good friend," said Flower. "We can trust her. You can use the living room."

"Thank you," said Carolynn.

Max Goodbody slowly stood, hiked up his navy-blue dress pants and tugged at the collar of his white Oxford. "I don't know why you want to speak with me in private. I have no secrets."

"Of course he doesn't," said Jill Goodbody, looking frightened.

"You don't have to talk with her, daddy," said Mink.

"It's all right," he said, patting Mink's arm.

Carolynn walked ahead of Max into the living room. Sunlight shone through the wide front window and made a trail across the rust-colored carpet. She sat on the couch while he sat just across from her in a gold chair. She could see sweat on his upper lip. She smiled at him, but he didn't relax. "I promised Holly I'd help her aunt," Carolynn said by way of explanation.

"I don't know what I can tell you." He narrowed his brown eyes and rested his left ankle on his right knee. His black shoes needed polishing.

"I just learned that you flew to Grand Rapids Thursday morning."

He dropped his foot to the floor and leaned forward in surprise. "So?"

"Did you go see Mink at Flower's place while Pete Chute was there?"

"What if I did?"

"Did you mention it to Sheriff Cobb?"

Max sank back in the chair. "No," he said hoarsely.

"Why not?"

"I didn't want him to suspect me."

"I can understand that." Carolynn set her purse beside her and leaned toward Max. "Was Pete alone when you saw him?"

"Alone?"

"Flower was gone or she would've said you were there. But Mink wouldn't want to involve you. Was she there when you were?"

Max sighed heavily. "No. Pete was alone in the kitchen."

"How did you get in?"

"How?"

"Yes."

"The back door."

"Did you have a key?"

"It was unlocked."

"Then what?"

Max cleared his throat. "I walked in the kitchen and Pete was there with M & Ms spilled on the floor, laughing at me because Mink was going to stay with him no matter what we said. I told him to leave her alone and that I'd call the police on him if he ever tried to beat her again. He laughed harder."

"Was Pete still in pain from Mink hitting him on the head?"

"He didn't seem to be."

"Then what?"

"I knew it wouldn't do any good to talk further. I left."

"Did you see the boning knife anywhere?"

"No. Flower said it had a special holder and nobody could see it."

"Did you tell Lavery what you told me?"

Max shook his head. "There was no reason to. But I would've if she'd asked me."

"I appreciate you taking the time to talk to me." Carolynn stood and so did Max. "I am very sorry about what Mink has gone through with Chute."

"Me too."

"I'm sure it was hard on both you and your wife."

"Yes." Max shuddered. "You have children so you know how we feel."

"I'd do anything to keep my kids from being hurt by someone else."

"Me too."

"But not kill someone."

Max shook his head. "No."

Carolynn thanked him again and they walked to the kitchen.

Later, in her car, Carolynn flipped open her notebook to what Flet had said about the morning of the murder. "Somebody's lying," muttered Carolynn. "Fletcher Raabe or Max Goodbody?"

She drove home, mulling over what each man had said. She pulled into her garage, but instead of going home to make dinner like she knew she should she walked to Flet's house. She rang his doorbell and waited a good five minutes.

"Are you home, Flet?" She rang the doorbell again, waited a few more minutes, then walked slowly back home.

Chapter 14

The phone was ringing as Carolynn walked in the house. She ran to answer it and her accompanist, Barbara, said, "Carolynn, I need you immediately to practice the songs for next week's wedding. Something came up and this is the only time I have free this week. I tried off and on all day to get you."

"Sorry, Barbara. I've been busy." Carolynn knew Barbara would never believe that. Since she was home most of the time everyone assumed that left her free to help in any situation. "I really should make dinner."

"I know it's terrible for me to take you away from your family now, but I just can't help it."

Carolynn sighed. Barbara sounded desperate. "I'll be there in a few minutes. I'm wearing jeans and sneakers. Is that all right?"

"It's fine with me. It won't hinder your beautiful voice."

Carolynn laughed and hung up. She listened for sounds of Robert in the basement or Stan upstairs. She couldn't hear either of them, but she shouted just in case. "I'll leave a note," she muttered. She saw the note from Robert still on the refrigerator, so she scribbled her own message on his note and stuck it back in place, then dashed to the car.

Robert stood beside his pickup and smiled down at Raeleen Ost. Bob and Price flanked her as usual. Robert had just finished fixing the fence around the goat pen. He was hungry, but a little afraid to go home. He didn't know what to say to Carolynn, nor what she'd say to him. He looked across the yard at the goat pen. "That fence should hold those goats now."

"I'll check before dark," said Rae. She leaned heavily on her cane. She didn't want to tell Robert her hip hurt more than usual. He might make her go to emergency to have it X-rayed. If there was an emergency she at least had on her wig and a new pair of white cotton underwear.

"I'm glad you got that thing," said Robert, pointing to the necklace hanging on Rae's chest. "I'd be a little nervous about leaving you. I know you're not feeling quite up to par this evening."

"I'll survive," said Rae with a grin. She was not one to go on and on about what ailed her. It tired her right out to hear some of those old women who get a kick out of telling all their physical problems.

Robert flicked a fly off his arm. He'd wanted to tell her about his talk with Carolynn, but had kept it to himself when he saw she wasn't feeling as chipper as usual. He had to admit to himself that he hadn't said anything yet because he still had to sort it all out in his own mind. How could his wife lead a double life? Maybe *double life* was a little strong.

"You got a lot on your mind, don't you, Robert?"

He smiled weakly and nodded.

"I'm here if you want to talk."

"Thanks. I appreciate that." He opened his pickup door. Bob and Price leaped up, their ears pricked. "See you in the morning, Rae."

"You sure you want to bother?"

"I said I'd milk the goats in the morning, and I will."

"I've been thinking I might just sell them goats."

"You love them! Why should you sell them?"

"I can't take care of 'em like I should."

"I'll do it until you can."

Tears stung her eyes and she wasn't one to cry. She made sure Robert didn't see even a hint of the tears. What was she? A baby?

She watched him drive away, then slowly made her way to the house with Bob and Price flanking her. "You boys have it made what with having four legs each," she said. "Maybe I should get down and crawl again like a baby does. It might be easier to get around."

Inside, she pulled off her wig and dropped it on the table beside the salt and pepper shakers. It always felt good to get the wig off, like taking off a warm hat to let air cool her head. She poured dry dogfood in the dish for Bob and Price, washed her hands and fixed herself a peanut-butter-and-jelly sandwich and a glass of milk. When Ben was alive she always made a big meal — meat, potatoes (usually mashed), a vegetable, tossed salad and dessert. Ben loved his desserts, especially her special brownies with nuts.

"You know, Bob, Price, I just might make some brownies tonight. I don't have any nuts, but I could make 'em without. Robert might want one tomorrow when he comes. He won't care if they don't have nuts in 'em. Me neither. I'd like a brownie right now with a glass of cold milk. Nothing's better."

Bob and Price whined, then sank to the floor, watching her, listening to her as if they understood every word.

Robert walked into the house expecting to smell dinner, but all he smelled was a hint of Stan's aftershave. "Carolynn," Robert called. He walked to the bedroom. Carolynn's flannel shirt lay in a heap on the bed. He checked the kitchen table where she always left a note, but none was there. Pain shot through him and he cried aloud. Had she lied to him? Was there another man? Or had something dreadful happened to her while she was trying to solve the Chute murder?

He paced the kitchen, the living room, dining room, den, bedroom and back to the kitchen. He opened the refrigerator and closed it without looking in.

Maybe he should drive to Peg's to see if Carolynn was there with someone. A groan rose from deep inside him. He jangled his keys in his pocket. Maybe he should go see. Get this settled once and for all! He strode to his pickup, his legs heavy and his stomach knotted so tight it hurt.

Suddenly he knew beyond a shadow of a doubt he'd find Carolynn at Peg's with Dud.

With a growl, Robert backed out of his parking space and roared out of the driveway. He gripped the steering wheel so tight his knuckles ached. He slowed as he neared Peg's house. He frowned. Carolynn's car wasn't in the drive. No car was. "Sure. They pulled in the garage," he said hoarsely.

He stopped in the driveway almost against the garage. Sweat popped out on his face as he ran to the garage window and peeked inside. It was empty! He staggered back to the pickup, then just sat behind the wheel, staring straight ahead.

"Don't let Satan lie to you," Carolynn had said.

"Am I doing that?" muttered Robert around the hard lump in his throat. He dropped his forehead to his hands and groaned.

After a long time he drove home, parked the pickup and walked inside. The hum of the refrigerator and the tick of the antique clock were the only sounds he heard.

"Heavenly Father, help me." Robert's voice broke. He sank to his favorite chair in the den and covered his ashen face with his trembling hands.

Stan stood in Holly's kitchen and waited while she told Paige and Noah and the others that she'd be out for a while. Flower had agreed to watch the kids since she was there with Mink and her parents.

Stan brushed a hair off the sleeve of his jacket, then looked down at his dress pants and his newly polished shoes. He'd showered, shaved and changed, then paced his room and prayed until finally he had the courage to call Holly to ask if he could see her. She'd sounded hesitant, but she'd agreed.

"I'm finally ready," Holly said brightly as she walked into the kitchen with her dark purple jacket over her arm and her purse in her hand.

Stan couldn't take his eyes off her. She wore dark purple slacks, a bright multicolored silky blouse and flat shoes the same color as her slacks. Her eyes sparkled. Was it because of him? His pulse leaped at the thought. "You look beautiful," he said in a voice he managed to keep level.

"Thanks. So do you." She laughed and wrinkled her small nose at him.

He walked her to his car and opened the passenger door for her. He caught a whiff of her perfume and his pulse leaped again. He walked to his side, took a deep, steadying breath and slid under the steering wheel. "It's a beautiful evening," he said. "I think spring has finally arrived." Oh, what gems of dialogue! He should jot them down to use in one of his books!

"I'm thankful Aunt Flower brought Mink back to talk to the sheriff. Aunt Flower said he believed Mink." Holly didn't say the hair Carolynn had found on the bed in Flower's spare room helped convince the sheriff. "I feel like a weight has lifted off my shoulders!" Holly laughed as she twisted in the seat to watch Stan as he drove. "The sheriff no longer suspects Aunt Flower or me. It's a relief."

"When can Flower move back home?"

"When she wants. But she's a little hesitant about it. It's pretty awful having a man murdered in your very own kitchen with your very own boning knife."

"I can imagine."

"I'm glad you called to take me out. Where're we going?"

Stan stopped at a stop sign and grinned sheepishly. "I never thought that far ahead."

"How about the park? It's such a nice evening. We could walk in the park, then go have something to eat."

"I like that." He felt his courage drain away as he pulled into the park and parked next to a white Buick.

"Oh, look! There's Paul!" Holly rolled her window down and waved, and Paul waved back.

Stan scowled. His fingers felt implanted in the steering wheel. Had she suggested coming because she knew Paul was there?

She slipped out of the car as Paul ran up. "Hello," she said. She was very glad to see him.

"Hi, Holly." Paul leaned down and peered in the window. "How are you, Stan?"

"Still hanging in there," said Stan even though he wanted to tell Paul to get lost.

Jealousy shot through Stan and his face and neck burned with white-hot rage. But he just sat there and watched Holly and Paul talk and laugh. Finally Paul walked away. Holly frowned in the window at Stan.

"Are you going to sit there all day?" she asked.

"I might," he said coldly.

"Are you jealous?" she asked in surprise.

"I have every right to be," he snapped.

She jerked open the door and slipped inside. "Don't be such a baby. I was only talking to the guy. We're friends."

Stan turned his head and stared out of his window. Several teenagers with a volleyball walked past, laughing and yelling. A horn honked. The smell of grilling hamburger drifted in Holly's window.

"Well?" she said finally.

He was suddenly too tired to think straight. "I guess I'd better take you home."

"Why?"

"You can't want to be around me when I'm being such a baby."

"You're right about that. Grow up! You're not a teenager, afraid of what's going to happen the next minute or hour or day. So act like it."

A muscle jumped in Stan's jaw. "I'm having a hard time here, Holly."

"I know. But you're going to do this on your own, Stan Burgess!"

"Do what on my own?"

"Do you think I was born yesterday? I know you have something on your mind and I know you're having a lot of trouble telling me what it is. If you can't tell me, take me home and let me have my dinner. I'm hungry."

He frowned at her. "you're not very romantic, are you?"

"Should I be?"

"I'm trying to tell you I love you!"

Holly sank back in her seat and stared at him. "And I thought you were going to tell me you were afraid we were getting too close. I though you were tired of me."

"Tired of you? I love you!"

She covered her burning cheeks with her hands and burst into tears.

He looked helplessly at her. If he were writing a story he'd know exactly what to have his character do and say, but in real life it was hard to know. Finally he reached for her and slowly gathered her close. "Don't cry, Holly. I didn't mean to upset you."

"I've...been so on...edge."

"I know. But you said things were almost back to normal."

She sniffed and pulled away from him. "Do you really...love me?"

He nodded. Suddenly he realized he'd told her and he'd survived.

"I mean *love* me?"

He ducked his head and laughed. She was almost as uncertain as he was! That was a real shocker. Finally he pulled her close. "I mean love you like a husband loves a wife. I love you," he said against her mouth, then he kissed her just as he'd done a thousand times in his daydreams.

Carolynn rubbed her throat as she walked into the quiet house. She felt as if she'd practiced for hours. She stopped in the kitchen with a frown. Robert hadn't even fed himself a sandwich to tide him over until she cooked dinner. "Robert? Are you in here?" She'd seen his pickup outdoors, but there were no sounds of TV or the stereo. She walked back to the bedroom. Maybe he was taking a nap. "Robert?" Only her flannel shirt lay on the bed.

A chill ran down her spine. Why wasn't he answering her? She walked slowly through the house and stopped in the den doorway. He sat in his chair with his head in his hands. "Robert?" she said softly.

Slowly he lifted his head. She saw by his eyes that he'd been crying. She felt an icy chill creep over her.

"What is it?" she asked as she knelt down beside him, her hands on his leg. "Did something happen to Raeleen Ost?"

"Where've you been?" he asked hoarsely.

"Practicing with Barbara. I left you a note."

He frowned. "I didn't see it."

"I wrote under your note on the refrigerator."

He cupped her face in his hands and kissed her a long searching kiss. "I love you, Carolynn," he whispered.

"I love you," she said, wondering about his strange behavior.

He dropped his hands from her and looked down at the carpet. "I did a very stupid thing."

She bit her bottom lip and waited. What had he done that upset him so much?

"I...drove to Peg's...to catch you and Dud together."

Carolynn sank to the floor, her mouth open in shock.

Robert jumped to his feet and paced the floor. His gray hair stood on end. He looked older than his years. "I couldn't believe myself!"

Carolynn pulled her knees to her chin and wrapped her arms around her knees. Was this her Robert? He had never been jealous before! Had she done this to him by keeping her work a secret? "I don't know what to say," she whispered.

"Neither do I." He dropped back in his chair, leaned his elbows on his knees and buried his face in his hands.

Fletcher Raabe forced the lock to the back entrance of Vital Call and slipped inside. He'd learned they had no alarm system and it was as if it was meant for him to break in. He flashed the flashlight around and the beam danced across the floor and over the walls. He opened one door to find it was the bathroom. It smelled as if it had just been cleaned. Two other doors led to empty rooms. He frowned, suddenly afraid he'd waited too long. He trembled and the light bobbed. He had to find evidence that they were working a scam so the authorities would shut them down and lock the crooks in jail and throw away the key.

The third door he opened had a desk, chair, and a few packed boxes inside. A computer sat on the desk. The floor creaked as he walked to a box sitting on a chair. He felt as calm as if he was home planning the job. This was something he had to do in order to get on with his life. He lifted the lid. It held several necklaces with red buttons. He checked another box and found a stack of agreements. He saw a box of floppy disks, but passed them up. What good would they do him since he had no computer to read them from?

A door closed and he heard men's voices. He froze. This hadn't been part of his plans. Suddenly he realized just what he was doing — breaking and entering. He could go to jail for that. Or worse, they could kill him. He heard the men getting closer, arguing about plans they'd made. Flet's heart hammered so loudly he was sure they'd hear it. He clicked off the light and tried to decide what to do. His brain seemed frozen.

Suddenly the overhead light flashed on and he blinked in the brightness. Fear kept him rooted to the spot.

"What's going on here?" growled Moran, his eyes wide in surprise.

"How'd you get in here?" asked Tremayne gruffly. He took a menacing step toward Flet.

Suddenly the fear left Flet and white-hot anger rose in him. He lifted his chin and his nostrils flared. "Do you think you can get away with murder?" asked Flet angrily.

"Murder? What're you talking about?" asked Tremayne.

"Get out of here!" snapped Moran.

Flet shook his head. "I'll hound your steps until I can prove you killed my wife." He looked right at Tremayne. "And your partner Peter Chute. It was you who did it, wasn't it?"

'You don't know what you're talking about," snapped Moran.

"The police will want to hear all of my story," said Flet. "I only told them a part of it because I knew they wouldn't believe me without proof."

"You seriously think we're going to let you out of here to cause trouble?" Suddenly Tremayne socked Flet in the chin and knocked him to the floor.

"That's a little drastic, isn't it?" asked Moran in surprise.

"He'll make too much trouble for us. We'll lock him in Chute's office and let him rot in there," said Tremayne.

The men lifted Flet and carried him down the hall to the door across from the bathroom. They dropped him in a heap on the floor, then walked out, muttering angrily. Moran locked the door and slipped the key in his pocket.

A few minutes later, Flet groaned and sat up. He tried to stand, but his head hurt too much and he was too dizzy. He leaned against the wall and groaned.

Rae watched the goats settle down for the night, then slowly she walked back to the house, the collies in their usual places beside her. It was just turning dark. A pleasant breeze blew against her. She was glad for the warmth of her coat and wig. "Bob, Price, we made it through one more day." She leaned heavily on her cane and slowed her steps even more. It wouldn't do to step in a hole and fall. Even if she had on her wig and her new underwear, there was no way she'd push the red button on the dumb necklace.

Just as she reached the back steps, her hip gave way and she buckled, tried to catch herself, but sprawled to the ground. She moaned in pain. Bob and Price whined down at her. Bob nudged her with his long nose.

"I'm still alive, boys, so don't look so scared." She tried to pull herself up, but the pain was so great her head spun. "Just let me lay here a bit, then I can crawl inside."

Whining, Bob and Price sank down, one on either side of her.

She couldn't believe she was actually sprawled on the ground like a tossed-out dishrag. Why couldn't she get up and get inside where she belonged? She was going to miss that show she'd planned to watch. She tried to remember what it was, but the pain in her hip kept her brain from working right.

After a long time, Rae lifted her head. So far so good. She moved. Pain shot through her hip. Sweat popped out on her face and bile filled her mouth until she was afraid she was going to upchuck right there, with Bob and Price looking on. She sank back down, more on her back than her side. "I don't know if I can make it, boys."

They whined. Bob licked her face. Price nudged her with his nose.

"I hate for you to see me this way." Her voice broke and she scowled. "I better not break down and cry like a baby."

With all the strength in her, she tried again to move. With a moan, she sank back down.

"Boys, I don't want to do it, but I got to push the dumb red button." Slowly she reached for it, hesitated, then pushed it. She knew if she didn't answer the operator they'd call Robert and an ambulance. "Robert will know what to do," she said. "I'll just lay here and Robert will come. He might make it before the ambulance. I hope so. I don't want to ride in no ambulance alone with strangers. They might take off my wig. Then where would I be?"

She settled down as comfortably as she could on the cold ground. "Boys, you move in close and keep me warm. Robert'll be here soon." She tugged her coat together the best she could, but she was lying on it and couldn't close it around her. The cold ground seeped through her coat, overalls, long johns and her new cotton underwear. She shivered. Bob and Price pressed in close on either side of her and she smelled their bad breath and dusty coats. "You boys need a breath mint. And a bath!"

Total darkness fell and stars came out. An owl screeched. Rae groaned. "Boys, where can Robert be? And that ambulance? I don't hear it roaring down my road, do you?"

The cold seeped into the very core of her being. The pain in her hip throbbed until her whole body was racked with pain.

Price touched his cold nose to her cheek and whined, then laid his head across her chest. She felt a little warmer.

Tears welled in her eyes and she tried to force them back, but they kept coming. They ran down her face. Bob licked them away. "I don't want you boys to see me cry," she whispered. "I don't do much crying."

After a long time she said, "God, Robert tells me you care about me." The words were barely a whisper. "I'm sure glad about that. I need somebody to care right now." Her voice broke and she swallowed. "I'm in a real pickle. Could you help me? This dumb red button didn't help a bit. But you're bigger than this dumb red button." She turned her face into Bob's dusty coat. "I sure do need you, God. I sure do."

She listened again for the sound of Robert's pickup or the ambulance. She didn't hear either. Not a car drove past, not even a kid on a bicycle.

After a long time, she whispered, "God, just in case I don't make it through the night I need to know I'll wake up in heaven with you. Jesus, forgive my sins and make me yours. And don't let Robert take my dying hard." She trembled. "He'll want to blame himself for talking me into buying this dumb Vital Call. Don't let him. Thanks, God." She was quiet a long time. "God, don't let my kids fight over my stuff. And see that my goats get a good home." She bit her bottom lip and sniffed. "I sure did want to see them bluebirds build their nests."

Chapter 15

Robert woke up with a start. What had awakened him? It was only five. Carolynn was still sound asleep and snoring. He slipped out of bed and stood there in the dark, listening. Something was wrong. He knew it. But what? If it were one of the kids, they'd call. And if it was Rae, she'd call or the special operator would.

"Heavenly Father, take care of whatever it is," he prayed under his breath.

Robert used the bathroom, splashed water on his face, then wandered into the kitchen. The floors creaked. The light from the microwave clock looked bright in the semi-darkness of the room. He opened the refrigerator, but closed it again. He hadn't eaten dinner last night, nor did he feel like eating now. He thought of Carolynn and pushed the thought abruptly away. He still couldn't sort out his feelings, nor come to grips with the life she'd led all these years. Last night he'd bared his heart to her, but he hadn't been ready to talk their situation out and reach a conclusion.

With a ragged sigh he walked back to the bedroom.

"Since I'm up I'll head out to Rae's and get done early," he muttered as he pulled on his jeans and sweatshirt. Suddenly a sense of urgency washed over him and he knew he couldn't take time to shave. Rae wouldn't care. Things like that don't bother her. He picked up his boots and pulled socks from his drawer. He'd put them on in the kitchen so he wouldn't wake Carolynn.

Outside, the air was crisp and the ground heavy with dew. Early morning traffic sounds reached him from the expressway five blocks away.

Several minutes later he drove into Rae's driveway. The lights in the kitchen and on the back porch were on. He frowned. Was Rae up so early? She usually wasn't this early of a riser.

He stepped from the pickup and his stomach knotted. Something was wrong. He could feel it. Birds twittered in the trees. Just then he heard the collies whine from near the back porch. "Why would Rae put the dogs out so early?"

Zipping his jacket against the chill, Robert hurried toward the back porch, then stopped when he saw the collies near the steps. Something lay between them, but it was too dark to make it out. His heart turned over. Suddenly he knew what it was. With a low moan, he ran to Rae and knelt near her head. "Bob, Price, let me help her," he said gruffly. Tears burned his eyes.

The collies whined, but stood slowly and stepped away from Rae, but stood guard.

Robert bent over her. "Rae? Can you hear me, Rae?" Why hadn't she pushed the red button?

She moaned and relief weakened him. She was alive!

"Rae, it's Robert. I'm here. You're going to be all right."

He moved her coat and found her hand curled around the special necklace. He jabbed the red button, then for good measure, jabbed it again. He wanted to pick her up and carry her inside, but he knew it wasn't safe to move her. "Rae, I have to get a blanket for you. I'll be right back." He pushed himself up. "Bob, Price, stay with her." They once again took their places next to her.

Robert ran into the house and grabbed two blankets from the foot of Rae's bed. He covered her carefully. Her coat and wig were wet with dew. Robert trembled as he realized that she'd been out all night long. If she'd walked out only a few minutes ago, her coat wouldn't be so wet.

"Rae, the ambulance will be here soon," he said, trying to sound calm and assured.

Rae's eyes fluttered open. "Dumb button don't work," she said hoarsely. "I pushed it last night."

Anger shot through Robert and he ran back into the house and dialed the emergency ambulance service, gave the information, then grabbed a heavy towel and a hat, then ran back to Rae. "Your wig is soaked, Rae. I have to take it off, but I brought the hat you wear in the winter." He talked to her as he eased off her wig, dried her head and slipped the hat on over her ears. He stayed hunkered down beside her, unwilling to move away even to sit on the step.

"I knew you'd come," said Rae weakly. "But I didn't know if I'd be here to see you."

"I'm glad you are. I'm not ready to say good bye to you."

A few minutes later they heard the siren, then saw the flashing lights of the ambulance.

"They're coming, Rae," said Robert with a quiver in his voice. "Thank God!"

With Bob and Price beside him, Robert watched as the paramedics checked Rae. He asked for the necklace and they slipped it off her and gave it to him. He gripped it tightly as they lifted her onto the stretcher. Bob and Price whined and moved in close to Rae.

"Bob, Price, go lay down," said Rae weakly.

They cocked their heads, then walked a few feet away and sank down.

Robert patted Rae's shoulder. "I'll be right behind you, Rae. When I see you're settled in the hospital, then I'll come back here and milk the goats. I'll take care of Bob and Price, too."

She smiled weakly, but couldn't speak.

Robert ran to his pickup and waited for the ambulance to pull out of the drive. He looked at the necklace on the seat beside him. "Those folks at Life, Inc. will hear about this," he said grimly.

Flet moved restlessly, then slowly opened his eyes. Every bone in his body ached from sleeping on the cold, hard floor. He looked at his watch. It was almost eight o'clock. From watching the place, he knew Floy Tedmund would be in soon and the men shortly after. Just how long would they keep him locked up? Or had they totally vacated the offices and left him to die? Shivers ran down his spine. He wasn't ready to die!

He limped to the door and rattled the knob, then rapped loudly. "Let me out! Help! Let me out right now!"

He listened, but all he heard was the distant roar of a truck.

With a whimper, he eased himself to the floor, wrapped his long bony fingers around his wide suspenders and leaned weakly against the wall beside the door.

Carolynn listened grimly on the bedroom phone to Jay Sommers. He'd learned the people at Life, Inc. were indeed packed and ready to move. He'd looked over the data discs he'd found in one office and opened the files right there on the laptop computer. He'd printed out information that he thought Carolynn would want, one thing being the list of names of customers.

"I plan to be at Life, Inc. when they open their doors this morning," Carolynn said. "Thanks for your help, Jay."

"No problem. Just remember you owe me one when I need you. Either today or tomorrow."

"I know." Carolynn said good-bye and hung up, then just sat on the edge of her bed and stared into space. She'd thought this was her last case, but she'd promised help to Jay. What would Robert do and say about that? "Why does life have to be so complicated?" she muttered.

Finally she made the bed and put on her makeup. She'd showered earlier and had eaten breakfast alone. She knew Robert would avoid her until he had it settled in his mind on what he wanted to say. She also knew he'd gone to help Rae. After that he'd bury himself in the basement with his birdhouses. Carolynn picked up her lipstick. Maybe she should storm the basement and demand they talk. "A lot of good that would do. It would take a stick of dynamite to blow words out of his mouth when he doesn't want to speak."

Several minutes later Carolynn parked on the street a half a block from Life, Inc., as close as she could get. She glanced at the Bluebird Cafe. Maybe it was having a special on grease-sopped fried eggs.

She squared her shoulders and walked into the building and toward the door marked Life, Inc. She tugged the jacket of her light-blue, tailored suit over her slacks, then touched the broach at the neck of her tailored white blouse. She'd curled her hair and brushed it away from her face. Today she was Jane Withy. If her plan worked, today would be the end of Life, Inc. She narrowed her eyes and gripped her black purse tightly. Floy wouldn't know what to do with her.

Taking a deep breath, Carolynn pushed open the door and sailed into the plush office. Floy sat behind her desk, the phone to her ear. She glanced up and her black eyes widened. She wore a gold and green dress that looked as if it had cost her a small fortune.

"I came to see Mr. Moran and Mr. Tremayne," said Carolynn briskly. "It's vital!"

"Just a moment, please," Floy said into the phone in her perfect voice. She pushed a hold button and smiled icily at Carolynn. "Both men are very busy."

"They'll want to see me."

"Oh?"

"I changed my mind. I want my mom to have Vital Call."

"I'll speak to Mr. Moran." Floy pushed another button on the phone. "Jane Withy is here to see you. She wants to have you connect Vital Call up for her mother after all."

"Tell him I'll come to his office," said Carolynn, starting around Floy's desk.

Floy jumped up and blocked Carolynn's way. "I'm sorry, but he's having work done on it and no one is allowed back there."

"I won't mind a little mess." Carolynn tried to duck around Floy, but she stood in her way, her eyes flashing angrily.

"Linus will be right out," said Floy coldly. "Take a seat. Please."

Carolynn shrugged and started to turn, then brushed past Floy.

"Stop!" cried Floy.

Mr. Tremayne's office door burst open and both men stepped out, blocking Carolynn's way. She frowned, but knew she couldn't handle both the men and Floy at the same time.

"Jane," said Mr. Tremayne, taking her arm firmly. "Let's sit over there and talk."

She sat on a chair under the picture she'd admired so much before and Tremayne sat beside her. Moran stood at Tremayne's side.

"I decided it would be better for mom to have Vital Call," said Carolynn. She cleared her throat and gripped her purse on her lap. "But I want to make a deal with you that will mean much more money for you."

Tremayne arched his brow. "Oh?"

"We're not in the market for deals," said Moran.

"We can listen," said Tremayne.

Floy folded her hands on her desk beside a heavy glass vase and leaned forward. She was ready to listen too.

Carolynn fingered her purse strap. "Can I trust all three of you? I mean, I don't want what I'm going to say to be spread around."

Moran moved restlessly as he glanced at his watch.

Tremayne smiled, but the smile didn't reach his dark eyes. "You certainly can trust us. We did give back the money your mother gave us for the system even though we didn't have to."

"That's why I think I can speak freely." Carolynn took a deep breath. "My mother doesn't live like it, but she has a small fortune tucked away in several banks."

"We shouldn't be listening to this," said Moran. "Weldon, didn't you say we have an appointment at ten?"

"It can wait." Tremayne smiled at Carolynn again. "Linus is a little on edge this morning. Please continue."

Carolynn moistened her pink lips with the tip of her tongue. "I need money desperately, but mom won't part with any of hers. She says I'll get it soon enough when she dies.'

"I don't like this at all," said Moran, dabbing his face with his hanky.

"It's really nothing that will harm you," said Carolynn. Butterflies fluttered in her stomach, but she didn't let it show. "I'd like to have you connect Vital Call again for mom. But when something happens to her, and I know something will, if you know what I mean, don't send help to her. When she presses the red button have the operator answer, but don't send an ambulance or make a call to me. No one will ever know what happened."

Moran groaned, Floy cleared her throat, and Tremayne laughed nervously. "Is this a joke?" he finally asked.

Carolynn shook her head. "You see, I already know that's how you operate your business."

"What?" cried Floy.

Tremayne scowled at her and she sank back in her chair. "What makes you say that?" he asked softly.

"I'm going to leave," said Moran.

Tremayne stopped him with a look.

Carolynn brushed a strand of hair back. "I tried out the system before I returned it."

"Maybe there was a malfunction," said Tremayne.

Carolynn smiled. "Like with Marj Raabe. I heard about that through the grapevine. And you know news travels fast that way. I could make it travel even faster if you don't do what I asked."

Floy jumped up. "I think we should kick her out now before she makes more trouble!"

Tremayne waved a hand at Floy, but kept his eyes on Carolynn. "It might be called murder, you know."

Carolynn shook her head. "No! It would be an accident."

"It is murder," said Moran grimly.

"Because she's my mother?" asked Carolynn angrily. "Marj Raabe was someone's mother. And wife. Wasn't that murder?"

Tremayne scowled at Moran, then patted Carolynn's arm. "Let's keep calm. Why don't you tell us just how much money will come to us?"

"The usual amount for Vital Call."

Tremayne shook his head. "I'm afraid that wouldn't be enough. Linus? Floy?"

"I don't want to listen to this," said Moran.

Floy spread her hands. "I think we should get our fair share."

Carolynn sighed heavily, then named a sum that brought a sparkle to Tremayne's eyes. "Is it a deal?"

Tremayne nodded, then Floy did. Finally Moran shrugged.

Suddenly the door burst open and Robert stormed into the office right up to Floy's desk, Rae's necklace dangling from his hand. "I want to see the man in charge!" he roared.

Carolynn fell back with a gasp.

Tremayne jumped up and Moran backed away from Robert.

"I'll call the police," said Floy.

"Go right ahead," said Robert. He flung the necklace on her desk, then whirled and grabbed Tremayne by the shirt front. Then he saw Carolynn. He stared at her in shock and his hand fell limply to his side. "Carolynn!"

"Robert, you'd better leave," she said weakly.

"Carolynn?" Tremayne and Moran said together.

Robert pulled his gaze away from Carolynn and turned it back to the men. He had important business to see to and he couldn't let Carolynn's presence deter him. He jabbed his finger at Moran, then Tremayne. "Raeleen Ost almost died because of your phony Vital Call system! Your phony business is over as of this minute. I'll call the police myself." He turned to reach for Floy's phone.

Tremayne caught Robert's arm and flung him away from the desk.

Floy gasped.

Carolynn stared at Robert as if she'd never seen him before.

Robert swung at Tremayne, but he blocked the blow with his muscled arm.

Carolynn jumped to her feet. "Robert!"

He swung again, this time hitting Tremayne in the stomach.

Moran jumped at Robert, hitting him in the side of the head. Robert staggered.

Suddenly Carolynn leaped into action. She kicked high at Moran, catching him in the shoulder. He staggered away from Robert. Before Moran caught his balance, Carolynn grabbed his arm and flipped him high. He landed with a thud on his back. He didn't move again.

Robert jabbed at Tremayne, then dodged away from Tremayne's fists.

From the corner of her eye, Carolynn saw Floy kick off her high-heeled shoes and leap forward, her hands in position to strike a karate blow. Carolynn spun and kicked, but Floy leaped out of the way.

They circled each other, watching for an opening.

Just then Robert landed a blow on Tremayne's chin that knocked him unconscious to the floor. Robert turned and saw Carolynn and Floy ready for battle. Floy was years younger than Carolynn, but that didn't seem to bother Carolynn. She looked like she knew what she was doing. And she looked in excellent shape.

Robert grabbed the vase from Floy's desk and flung it at her, then when she knocked it aside, he stepped in and punched her in the chin. She sprawled on the floor beside the desk. He caught up the phone cord and wrapped her ankles and wrists before she could move.

Carolynn stared at him in shock. When had he learned to fight like that?

He turned to Carolynn, his nose bleeding and his breath short. "Are you all right?"

She nodded weakly. "Are you?"

"I'll know in a minute." He sank to a chair, his chest rising and falling. He fumbled for his hanky and held it to his nose.

"I'll take care of these two and call the police," said Carolynn, suddenly all business again. She ran to Tremayne's office, found strapping tape and quickly bound Tremayne and Moran who were both groaning in pain. With Robert's help she lined the three of them up against the wall. She called Sheriff Farley Cobb from Tremayne's office and he said he'd be right there.

As she stepped out of his office she heard a loud thud from the office down the hall. She frowned, then decided to investigate. The key was in the lock. She hesitated, then unlocked the door and peered inside. Flet lay on the floor bound with strapping tape and gagged with a scarf. "Flet!" She ran to him and quickly set him free.

Tears filled his eyes and he couldn't speak.

Carolynn patted his shoulder and smiled. "You're all right now, Flet. And this business is closed for good."

Flet awkwardly rubbed away his tears. "I think Tremayne is the one who knocked me down at Flower's house. I think he killed Pete Chute."

"You could be right," said Carolynn. "Let's go ask him."

They walked together to the others. Robert looked at Flet in surprise while he told what had happened to him last night, then about Tremayne tying him up and gagging him when he came in this morning.

Carolynn stood beside Tremayne and looked down at him. "Flet here thinks you killed Peter Chute."

"What? I did not!"

"You'd better have an air-tight alibi or Sheriff Cobb will arrest you for it," said Carolynn.

Tremayne scowled and tried to move. "I was with at least ten people at the Congregational Church, telling them about Vital Call that day," said Tremayne. "I can prove it."

"I'll believe it when I see it," said Carolynn. But she knew it would be stupid for him to lie about an alibi that could be checked so easily. He probably was telling the truth even though she'd hoped he wasn't.

"He's lying," said Flet, trembling as he stared down at Tremayne. "He did knock me out while I was talking to Chute."

Carolynn frowned slightly. "Flet, you said the man strangled you."

"I must've been thinking wrong. He knocked me out with something heavy. I still got the scab where the skin was broke." He rubbed the back of his head. He turned and bent down to Carolynn. "See."

She looked and saw the scab. "Then someone short could've hit you. You said a tall man grabbed you, knocked the knife from your hand and strangled you."

"I did?"

Carolynn's heart turned to ice. Why would Flet change his story? Had he killed Chute after all?

Robert laid his hand on Flet's shoulder. "Sit down and tell us what happened again, Flet. Sometimes things get fuzzy. Or it's embarrassing to tell the whole truth."

Carolynn stared at Robert in surprise as Flet sank to the chair under the flower picture. Carolynn leaned against Floy's desk and kept quiet. Floy and the men sat against the wall in defeat.

Flet shook his head, almost as if he was clearing his brain.

"Talk when you're ready," said Robert, patting Flet's shoulder.

Flet sighed heavily. "My thinking wasn't fuzzy, but I didn't tell Carolynn everything."

She bit her tongue to keep from asking why. it looked like Robert was going to learn the truth from Flet.

He told about getting into Flower's house through the back door and about his argument with Chute. "When he made me pick up them M & Ms I saw red," said Flet. "I got out Flower's special boning knife and I wanted to kill Chute, but he knocked it out of my hand, then hit me with that rock that Flower uses for a bookend to hold up her recipe books. When I came to, Chute was dead." He looked at Carolynn helplessly.

"I made up the part about a man coming in so you wouldn't think I killed Chute." He shook his head. "And I didn't!"

"And did you leave the back door open like you said?" asked Carolynn.

Flet nodded. "Somebody else killed Chute. Not me. I'm telling the truth, Carolynn."

"She believes you," said Robert. "Don't you, Carolynn?"

She hesitated, then finally nodded. Then who did kill Peter Chute?

Chapter 16

Carolynn stood beside Robert and Flet as Farley read their rights to Floy, Tremayne, and Moran. Carolynn, Robert, and Flet had already told the sheriff what they knew about Life, Inc. and how they came to be there.

Just as Farley finished, Lavery pushed past Deputy Kit Littlejohn and walked in. She looked shocked, then angry.

Carolynn sucked in her breath and wanted to find a way to disappear.

"What happened here, Sheriff?" asked Lavery in surprise.

"Police business," he said. "It doesn't concern you."

Just then Lavery spotted Carolynn and fire shot from her eyes. "You! How is it you're here, Burgess?"

Carolynn searched frantically for something to say.

"Kit, take these folks out to the car," said Farley, pushing Moran toward the deputy. He turned to the others. "Suppose you folks get on your way so we can lock up here. Raabe, I want you to come with me and answer a few more questions. The rest of you go about your business."

Carolynn breathed a sigh of relief as she walked out ahead of Robert. Her relief was short-lived as Lavery caught her arm and pulled her up short before she could leave the building.

"Just what did your snooping get you into this time, Burgess?" asked Lavery.

Carolynn tugged free of Lavery. "I guess I was there at the right time to see the action," Carolynn said with a smile.

Robert slipped his arm around Carolynn. "A friend of ours almost died because of those people. We came to put an end to the business."

"What friend?" asked Lavery sharply.

"Raeleen Ost," said Robert.

Carolynn hid her surprise. Robert was actually covering for her! She listened as he told Lavery about Rae. It didn't take Lavery long to excuse herself and walk away. Carolynn turned to Robert with a chuckle. "Thanks. She's very determined to prove I'm more than a secretary."

"I figured that," he said with a laugh.

Carolynn flung her arms around Robert and hugged him hard. "Maybe Dud should hire you."

Robert held her close. "Not me. I'm not cut out for that kind of work." He stepped back from her. "Just when did you learn self-defense?"

"A long time ago."

"I'm impressed."

"You are? I was pretty impressed with the way you handled yourself with those men and with Flet."

"I learned a few things down through the years." Robert rested his hand slightly on her shoulders and looked into her eyes. "I realized something this morning when I was sitting by Rae in the hospital."

Carolynn stood very still. "Oh?"

"There has to be people out there fighting crime to save the Raeleen Osts of this world. Why shouldn't you continue to be one of them if that's what you want?"

Carolynn's eyes filled with tears and her lip quivered.

"I feel bad that you didn't trust me enough to tell me years ago, but I know you were right. I would've been afraid for you to do something so dangerous."

She rested her hands on his chest and felt the thud of his heart. "I still should've told you, Robert. It wasn't right to keep part of me from you. We're one. And by keeping my secret life I tore us apart. And I always thought it was you because you wouldn't talk to me." She reached up and kissed him. "I love you, Robert."

Love for her rose inside him so strongly that he couldn't find words to say. He held her close to his heart and never wanted to let her go.

Reluctantly Carolynn pulled away from Robert. "Who did kill Peter Chute? Mink?"

"I have no idea. Why don't you tell me what you know and maybe we can figure it out together."

She gasped in surprise and delight. "Do you *know* how many times I've wanted to discuss my cases with you to get your input? Finally I can! Thank you, Robert! You'll never know how happy that makes me."

He smiled proudly. "Let's go eat lunch at the Bluebird Cafe and talk."

She wrinkled her nose. "The Bluebird Cafe?"

"They won't think a thing of a man walking in with blood on his shirt. I've eaten there many times when I was working construction. They make great reubens."

"Then let's go!"

Several minutes later, after eating a delicious reuben, drinking a cup of tea and telling Robert all she knew about Chute's death, Carolynn said, "Wait a minute! The M & Ms! I know who killed Peter Chute! I should've seen it before."

"Who?"

She leaned over and whispered in his ear.

"That's just who I was going to say! But what does candy have to do with it?"

"Let's get out of here. I have to call Farley and Holly."

Several minutes later, Carolynn parked outside Holly's house while Robert pulled up behind her in his pickup. They walked up the drive together. The sun shone brightly. Two robins hopped in the yard, then suddenly flew away. Music drifted out from a house across the street.

"Holly said she'd like Stan to be here, too," said Carolynn.

"They're pretty serious about each other, aren't they?"

"It wouldn't surprise me a bit if they got married."

"You've wanted that for them since high school."

Carolynn grinned with a shrug. "A mother's heart. What can I say?"

He leaned down so his mouth was close to her ear. "You're my heart."

Her pulse leaped and she squeezed his hand, then held it while they waited for someone to answer the door.

Flower opened the door, looking flustered. She wore a black dress with big red polka dots and earrings to match. "I don't understand why you wanted me to detain Mink and her parents," Flower whispered. "They're very anxious to leave."

"I'm sure," said Robert drily.

"Thanks for your help, Flower," said Carolynn. "Let's go talk to Mink and her folks while we wait for the sheriff."

Flower led Carolynn and Robert to the front room. Max and Jill sat on the couch, Mink on a nearby chair, and Stan and Holly on the raised hearth. "Look who's here," said Flower.

Carolynn waited until the greetings were over, then she said, as she and Robert sat on the love seat, "What happens now, Mink?"

Mink hooked her long hair behind her ears and smiled slightly. She wore jeans and a pull-over, pink sweater. "As soon as the sheriff says we can leave town, I'll go home with mom and daddy. Probably I'll get a job in Indianapolis and start a new life."

"I'm sure you're both happy about that, aren't you?" Carolynn asked Max and Jill.

They nodded. Max said, "I'm just glad she's free of Pete Chute!"

I'm sure you are. But not glad about murder. We know what happened," said Carolynn softly, looking right at Max.

He flushed.

"What do you mean?" asked Mink.

"Your dad should tell you," said Robert before Carolynn could speak. "It's better if he tells you."

"Daddy?"

"What is it, Max?" asked Jill.

Max cleared his throat. "I don't know what they're talking about."

"Chute's death," said Carolynn. She was glad Stan, Holly, and Flower didn't interrupt.

"What dad wouldn't want to protect his daughter?" said Robert.

"Daddy?" cried Mink.

Jill sank back and covered her ashen face with trembling hands.

Max stabbed his fingers through his hair.

"We know,' said Carolynn again.

Max sucked in his breath. "I didn't mean to kill him."

Mink burst into tears and Flower quieted her.

"Tell us about it," said Carolynn.

"When Mink called us to tell us she was staying with her friend Flower while she thought about leaving Pete I decided I'd go talk to her and convince her to walk away from him and not look back. I got there and knocked, but no one answered. I waited a bit, then walked to the back door. It was open, so I walked in. I heard Pete yelling at Fletcher Raabe. I learned later who he was. Pete hit the knife from the old man's hand, then knocked him out." Max shuddered. "I grabbed the knife and Pete told me to drop it. He said nothing would make him let Mink go. He sprang at me and I thrust the knife out. It caught him in the chest and he fell back. I didn't mean to kill him. I just wanted him to quit hurting my little girl."

Carolynn watched as Mink and Jill wrapped their arms around Max and they all cried together. Carolynn caught Holly's eye and barely nodded.

Holly moved her head a fraction. She was glad Carolynn had solved the case, but she hated to learn Max was the killer.

Several minutes later the sheriff drove away with Max while Jill and Mink followed in their car.

"Now I can go home," said Flower. "I can tell Lavery I no longer need her services. And I can go back to work at the abuse center."

"Do you even want to?" asked Holly.

Flower nodded. "I must! I want to do all I can to stop what happened to Mink." She hugged Holly, said good bye to the others and walked outdoors to her red Corvette.

Holly pulled Carolynn aside while Stan took Robert to the kitchen for a glass of Diet Pepsi.

"Thanks for all you did, Carolynn," said Holly softly.

Carolynn shrugged. "I'm glad I could help."

"I was surprised Robert came with you."

"I told him about my work."

"Was he shocked?"

"Yes, but everything's all right." Carolynn tapped Holly's shoulder with her finger. "What about with you and Stan?"

Holly hugged Carolynn. "We're coming along. One step at a time."

"Good."

"Will you tell Stan about your work?"

"No. It's better for me to continue as I am."

"Then I won't tell him either."

"Thanks." Carolynn kissed Holly's cheek, then they walked to the kitchen to the men.

Stan slipped an arm around Holly and whispered, "I missed you."

Later at home Carolynn changed into jeans and a red plaid blouse while Robert talked to Rae on the phone.

Robert laughed as he hung up. "She's doing fine. Her roommate likes 'The Price Is Right' as much as she does. They both love animals and they're both widows with broken hips. She says she learned about a system similar to Vital Call that's legitimate and she's going to get it once she gets her money back from Life, Inc."

"Good. We'll take flowers to her later today," said Carolynn as she tied her sneakers.

"She wants to hear all the details about the downfall of Life, Inc." Robert caught Carolynn's hands in his. "Speaking about details, what did M & Ms have to do with solving the murder case?"

"Flet said he knocked the candy from Chute's hand and it spilled all over. He picked up some, but not all. When he regained consciousness he finished picking up the candy and left. Max said when he came in to talk to Chute he was all alone and candy was all over the floor. Somebody was lying. Not Flet, once you convinced him to tell the whole story."

"But M & Ms? How do you know they weren't lying about them?"

"Usually people don't lie about the small details. Why would either of them make up a story about the M & Ms?"

Robert ruffled Carolynn's hair. "You're pretty smart."

She wrinkled her nose at him. "I know." She tapped his chest. "So, how did you know who did it?"

"Gut feeling. I know what I'd feel like doing if someone beat Eleena or Christa."

"I'd feel the same if someone was beating Wes or Stan." Carolynn laughed as she punched Robert's arm. "Keep that in mind if you ever get angry enough to beat them."

"I will." He sobered and he pulled her tight against him. "I'm sorry you were afraid of my temper all these years. I'm working on it, you know."

"I know. Just like I'm working on sharing all my life with you."

Robert kissed her thoroughly. "Hey, before we have our 50th wedding anniversary we'll be perfect."

"I believe it," said Carolynn as she kissed him again.

About the Author

Hilda Stahl was born and raised in the Nebraska Sandhills with sand between her toes and wind in her hair. She walked the prairie, enjoying the vastness, and never once thought about writing or being a writer.

After accepting Christ into her life as a young teen she felt a great call from God to help others.

As a young wife and mother living in Michigan, Hilda knew she couldn't leave her family to be a missionary or an evangelist. One day she saw an ad for a correspondence course in writing and took it. Some days she'd only have minutes to write, but she wrote during those minutes. She studied books on how to write every opportunity she had. She wrote when the babies were in bed or in school. She wrote even when rejection slips piled high around her. She wrote when she was too tired to see. She wrote and she wrote, and then she began selling almost everything that she wrote. That's how this award-winning author of nearly 100 books and hundreds of short stories began touching hearts with God's love. She belongs to the Society of Children's Book Writers and is listed in many publications including *Foremost Women of the 20th Century, International Authors* and *Writer's Who's Who,* and *The World's Who's Who of Women.* Her books are published in several languages.

Today Hilda is one of America's best loved authors. Her stories combine mystery, adventure, romance and real-life conflicts. Her books help readers to handle situations in their own lives as well as show that God is always the answer.

Hilda and her husband, Norman, live in Michigan on eighty beautiful acres. They have seven fantastic children and seven blessed grandchildren.

Hilda Stahl had a dream that she would be a famous writer; the dream came true. She continues to write, to teach, and to speak, but mostly to write because that's what God has called her to do.